MAGNOLIA BLOSSOMS

RHONDA R. DENNIS

Magnolia Blossoms

Copyright © 2014 RHONDA R. DENNIS

ISBN: 0991386809
ISBN-13: 978-0-9913868-0-2

DEDICATION

For my fans. I love you all so much!

ACKNOWLEDGMENTS

Big thanks to Donette Freeman, editor extraordinaire! Thank you to Bookfabulous Designs for the spectacular cover! Your talent continues to amaze me, Laura. To those who believed in my quirky story and encouraged me to keep going with it—you are the reason Magnolia is here. Hayley, Jenny, Karly, Laura, Donette, Heather B., Brenda, Heather R., Caroline--you are just a small sample of the amazing women in my life. Thank you for all you've done to help me with this project.

one

You know that guy on the TV commercials—the rotund, obnoxious attorney who fervently strokes his long gray beard while sporting a seersucker suit and browline glasses? The one who promises to "get you the money you deserve faster than green grass through a goose?" Well, he's my father, Big Daddy. And the middle-aged woman whom people love gossiping about—the one with super long, curly blonde hair, the body of someone half her age, and offers the majority of her art classes while nude—that's my mother, Sunny.

What results when these larger than life personalities procreate? An overwhelmingly beautiful and outspoken extrovert? Nope. Instead, you get me, Magnolia Picasso Berrybush. Imagine going through elementary school with parents like mine AND the last name of Berrybush. The kids weren't very kind, so my self-preservation plan included blending into the background as much as possible. It's a plan that I still use to this day.

I should also mention that I'm incredibly thin, so thin that I've been told I have to stand up twice to make a shadow. A la beaver style, my oversized front teeth protrude well past my lower lip. My overbite was supposed to be fixed via orthodontia when I turned ten, but Jimmy Jenkins told me I'd never be able to leave the house when it rained because I'd attract lightning. It was a chance I wasn't willing to take; it rains a lot in South Louisiana. Of course I now know that he was being a jerk, but twenty-two years have gone by, and I'm still sporting buckteeth. Damn Jimmy Jenkins and his stupid lies.

My long, mousy brown hair is always in a tight bun directly on top of my head, and all I ever wear are turtlenecks, ankle length argyle skirts, and one of the three pairs of boots I own: one black, one brown, and one yellow rubber for the rainy days. It doesn't matter that the majority of our days are scorchers. That's all I wear.

Freckles dot my face, and I rarely shave my legs or armpits, not because I'm trying to make a statement, but simply because I'm lazy and I don't care. What's the point? I have no life. Never had a boyfriend—ever. I haven't a single friend either, but I'm okay with that. No one ever understands me, and I gave up trying figure out people a long time ago. I'm just fine living life with me, myself, and I.

I lace the strap of my overstuffed messenger bag between my nearly non-existent breasts then shut the door to my little apartment that sits over my parents' garage. With a white-knuckled grip on the handrail, I gingerly ease my way down the steep stairs. *One foot down, next foot, together. One foot down, next foot, together.* I always repeat that mantra whenever I descend stairs. Grateful for yet another successful voyage down my Mt. Everest, I smile as my heart rate returns to normal.

My parents' house is a huge turn- of –the- century home with a wraparound porch. The pillars are white, the siding is garishly yellow, and the trim is French Quarter green, another amalgamation of Sunny's and Big Daddy's distinct, yet dissimilar preferences. I enter their house through a side entrance, and I'm instantly greeted with bright, lemon yellow walls. Voices echo down the hall, so I assume Sunny is in the middle of an art lesson. Yep, the sunroom is filled with easels, canvases, saggy balls, and droopy boobies. It's a sight that I've unfortunately acclimated to, so I don't even blink as I pass the glassed-in room to make my way to the kitchen.

"Hello Magnolia, darlin'. What brilliant adventure does this day have in store for you?" Big Daddy roars. He never turns it off. He's always in full theatrical mode.

"Work," I softly answer, my back turned to him while filling my travel mug with coffee.

"That's nice. I'm off to court. Tell Sunny that

I'll likely run late today. My client was charged with—murder." He draws his fist closed, and after shutting his eyes, he plants his forehead on top of it. He sighs heavily. "I foresee quite a long and incredibly draining day." He snaps out of his "woe is me" routine and cheerily asks, "Magnolia, is Big Daddy's tie straight?"

"Yes, sir," I say, barely glancing his way.

"Excellent. Did you need anything before I go?" he asks, sliding file folders into his leather briefcase.

"Actually," I quietly begin. "I was hoping you could..."

"Good, good, good. See y'all tonight," he says, slamming his case shut before wobbling out of the door. I should probably be offended, but I've grown accustomed to being ignored, so it doesn't faze me. I cap my coffee, and after checking my watch, grab a handful of almonds. Once I have my ill-fitting, lavender-colored, daisy-adorned helmet strapped on, I sit on the seat of my bright yellow Vespa scooter—a gift from none other than Sunny. After I wrecked five different clunkers that Big Daddy called "starter vehicles," my parents decided that the world would be a much safer place without my being behind the wheel of a three thousand pound automobile. The scooter was my twenty-first birthday present. It makes the ride to my job at the Louisiana State Archives quite unpleasant most of the time, but it really is a public service for mankind in general.

Once I arrive at work, I make a beeline for the

4

break room where I deposit my lunch bag into a locker. My messenger bag stays with me. There is a small group of middle aged women cackling about some TV show they watched the night before, but they don't notice me. Intrigued by their descriptions, I make a mental note to do an internet search for Charlie Hunnam. I quietly hug the wall while ducking out the room.

My job isn't glamorous or fun, but it's not complicated or demanding either. I find a list of requested documents on my desk each morning, and I pull the requested records and route them where they're supposed to go. It generally takes my coworkers their entire shifts to finish their record requests. On average, I finish my list within two hours, but I'd never let them know that. After I'm done with my work, I forward my phone calls and retreat to my secret spot.

Passing shelf after shelf of books, I make my way to the very far corner of the building, then after assuring no one is around, I kneel and remove six of the huge volumes lining the bottom shelf. I toss my messenger bag inside the gap. Looking again to make sure I'm unnoticed, I climb through the hole and take refuge in my secret cubby. The little cave grows darker and darker as I replace the books. Once they are all back in their respective slots, I click on the flashlight velcroed to the upper part of the shelf. The little cubby illuminates, and I start to unpack my bag: an Ereader, an apple, a banana, peanut butter crackers, a praline, a bottle of water, dental floss, wet wipes, my cell phone, and a plastic bag. Reclining back on a pillow, I pull a coverlet, one that I keep stashed in the pillowcase, over my torso, and then I power up my Ereader. It opens to the place where I'd bookmarked the erotic novel purchased the night before.

Since I've never had a boyfriend, or any friend for that matter, the only information I have on sex comes from novels, TV shows, movies, or pornos I watch on my phone. With Sunny in the house, I was educated on the anatomy of the human body at a very young age, but sex is so much more than anatomy—at least that's what I conclude by watching and reading about it. I want to have sex—badly. However, I'm starting to feel that after thirty-two years of virginity, I'm officially trapped in a permanent, monogamous relationship with myself. At least I know what I like and what I don't like. If I needed to hurry, I make it happen. If I have more time, I work with that, too. Though pleasuring myself has its perks, I can't help but wonder how much different it will be with another person involved.

The alarm on my phone buzzes just as I'm getting to the end of the book. It's time to make my way to the break room for lunch. I used to skip lunch, but once upon a time, someone realized I hadn't been seen all day, and a massive search ensued. Luckily, I was able to pop out of my hiding spot and perform some damage control before things got too out of hand. As long as I check in during lunch, everyone tends to leave me be. After my peanut butter and jelly sandwich is consumed, I toss the remnants of the brown paper bag into the trash and make haste back to my secret spot. I remain there until three forty-five, after which I climb from my hiding spot, straighten my desk, undo the call forwarding, and I'm out the door for four.

Back home, Sunny has Tofurky and roasted veggies ready to go. I eat none of it; neither does Big Daddy. He usually comes home with a bucket of chicken or something. I don't eat that either. My diet is pretty much limited to fruit, peanut butter and jelly sandwiches, and pizza. Sitting across from Sunny, I push the food around my plate while watching her glance through the newspaper. She's still nude. Other than when she has to leave the property or when she sports the occasional muumuu, Sunny is never clothed. After what I predict is an acceptable amount of dinner non-consumption, I discard my meal, load the plate in the dishwasher, and give Sunny a quick peck on the top of the head before I leave for my garage apartment.

Going up the stairs is much easier for me than coming down, so I make quick work of getting to the top. I hit number one on my speed dial and order a small pepperoni pizza for delivery. After inhaling half of it, I take a shower, pull on a pair of worn out pajamas, then scroll the guide for anything that might hold my attention. Eventually, I drift off to sleep, and the next day, it all happens again.

RHONDA R. DENNIS

two

The only thing more boring than work days are weekends. Big Daddy and Sunny generally disappear to one of the casinos in Louisiana or on the Mississippi gulf coast, and they don't return until late Sunday evening. I went with them once, but after I packed up my things at the end of the weekend, it wasn't until I stood outside the Hard Rock Hotel for two long hours that I realized they had inadvertently left me behind. They apologized when they came back to get me, but the memory still freaks me out, and now I prefer to leave the road- running to them.

Saturday afternoon presents nothing to watch on TV, nothing to read, and nothing to eat, so I decide to break my routine and head to the Mall of Louisiana. Surviving the trip on my Vespa is an accomplishment in itself; Baton Rouge traffic leaves much to be desired. While meandering through the bustling mall, I occasionally stop to browse at some of the store fronts. I don't fuss or snap when people bump into me. I can't even begin to count the number of times that I hear, "Whoops! Sorry! Didn't see you there." When I'm knocked to the floor without the perpetrator so much as looking back to check on me, I begin to feel a new emotion stirring deep in my belly. Unsure of what to classify it as, I continue on to the food court.

Patiently waiting in line at the corn dog stand, I watch as customer after customer is served. I look away for a second, and next thing I know, a group of teenagers has cut ahead of me to claim a spot near the register.

"Uhm, excuse me," I say quietly while tapping the young man directly in front of me. "I was actually the next in line."

"Fuck off," he says without as much as a glance my way.

After taking a moment to assure I'd heard correctly, I tap his shoulder again. "Does your mother know that you use such foul language, especially to strangers? What you said was extremely rude and I think…"

He spins around to confront me. "Whatcha gonna do about it, Fugly?"

"I suppose there's nothing much I can do about it, and my name isn't Fugly."

He laughs loudly which catches the attention of the others. I'm suddenly in a sea of saggy pants and sideways ball caps. The ring leader continues to belittle and berate me until the manager catches wind of what they are doing and shoos them off. I score a free corn dog and a half priced lemonade. The unfamiliar feeling is back in the pit of my stomach, so I eat maybe half of my corn dog before tossing it into the trash. Ready to return to my safe haven, I leave the mall and head towards home.

There's a Starbucks about two miles from my house, and my stomach rumbles when I approach the drive. Dusk is approaching, but I'm sure I'll have time to grab a caramel macchiato and a scone before nightfall. I place my order and giggle like an idiot when the man behind the counter yells, "Magnolia! The beautiful state flower of the great state of Louisiana! Where are ya, beautiful Maggie? Your order is up!"

I approach the counter, and I receive a very disappointed, "Oh, you're Magnolia?" from him. He nods at my cup then disappears behind a machine.

I sink into a fluffy chair not far from two elderly women who, surprise, don't even notice me. One is staring at the news scrolling across the gigantic flat screen mounted high on the wall. The other is steadily giving her an earful of advice.

"Aren't you scared, Lyla? You should be terrified. That man has killed how many people and he's still on the loose! They call him the Dollar Devil because he always leaves behind a dollar bill skewered by a tiny pitchfork made of toothpicks. Isn't that the darndest thing you ever heard? I haven't had a good night's sleep since they announced the details about him. He went from a nobody to everyone knowing him overnight. I imagine it'll only be a matter of time before they catch him."

"From your lips to God's ears, Abigail. Yes, indeed. Scary times for our town."

They continue on with their conversation, but I lose interest. One phrase plays over and over in my mind. *He went from a nobody to everyone knowing him overnight.* That feeling that was in the pit of my stomach earlier—I finally identify it. I want to be someone! I'm tired of being ignored, overlooked, disregarded, and unnoticed. I've lived in the shadows for thirty-two years, and I'm sick of it! Serial killer? Most are male, so that in itself will surely boost my notoriety. The obvious downside is that I'll have to kill people to become a serial killer. Am I capable of doing that?

My eyes dart from side to side as I contemplate it. I think I can. Not just anyone though. They have to be really mean or really old, so it'll be like I'm doing them a favor by getting rid of them. What if I get caught? Prison isn't a very nice place; I've seen the TV shows and movies. Can't be any worse than the prison I live in now. That's it! I've made up my mind. I'm going to become a serial killer. Too bad I don't know where that little douche from earlier lives. He could be the first victim of...of... A name! I need a name.

I dash out of the store and hop on the Vespa. Time to start making plans!

****

With a pencil tucked behind each ear and a notebook opened to page one, I lie on my stomach kicking my raised feet together as I repeatedly engage then retract the tip of my ballpoint pen. *Name:* I write in the first line. *Red Daisy.* I crack a smile. I decide to draw a daisy with red lipstick on my victims' foreheads. Brilliant! Pulling my laptop within typing distance, I research everything from methods to motives. I decide that my first victim will be very old, so there will be less of a fight. As I gain experience, I'll move towards something more challenging. I jot a few more notes then hop into bed. Lipstick shopping tomorrow!

I shower, shoot a spray of deodorant under each pit, then wind my hair into as tight a bun as comfortable. White cotton briefs, green turtleneck, brown argyle skirt, and brown boots complete my wardrobe. After my "one foot down, next foot, together" routine, I dash into the main house for a cup of coffee and some peanut butter toast. I'm surprised to find Sunny at the kitchen counter.

"Is something wrong? Why are you back so early?" I ask my mother. I should probably be grossed out by the sight of her whisking a bowl of eggs in the nude, but I'm used to it.

"That murder trial that Big Daddy has been working on is taking longer than expected. He's going over some case files in his office," she answers, putting down the bowl to tie an apron around her waist. Her boobs poke out either side of the bib, so she works to tuck them in.

"No soysage today?" I ask, placing my empty coffee mug into the dishwasher.

"Big Daddy prefers crispy swine belly to healthy, nutritious soy today. Who am I to argue? The soul of that poor pig will likely haunt him, but he doesn't care. Heartburn, flatulence, indigestion: all the result of animal souls searching for release from the confines of the nasty gastrointestinal tracts of the humans who have consumed them. Do carrots cry when you pick them? No. Do cucumbers scream when you pluck them from their vines? Have you ever heard the sounds animals make when they are slaughtered? It's not pleasant, Magnolia. Not pleasant at all."

Sunny was speaking of animals, but it reminds me that I hadn't considered that my victims might make sounds when I off them. That would be terrible! What if someone cried out for help or made vile gurgling sounds as they died. My stomach flips. I might need to rethink my path to infamy.

Sunny pulled me from my thoughts. "Are you going into town later?" she repeats after she realizes I hadn't heard her.

"Yes, ma'am," I answer softly. "I thought I would."

"Great! Will you stop into Mr. Gaine's shop for

me? He has a few supplies on hold, and he closes soon. The last thing I want to do is go into town smelling like bacon."

"Sure, Sunny. I'll do it," I say, placing the strap of my messenger bag across my body.

"Good girl," she says, her nose scrunched with disgust as she adds a few more strips to the sizzling pan.

My first stop is to the drug store, where after nearly an hour of browsing the makeup section, I select Assassin's Kiss as The Red Daisy's signature lipstick shade. Step one was complete. I smile broadly the entire five minute ride to Mr. Gaine's art supply shop. He wasn't just old; he was downright ancient, slow as molasses, and nearly blind and deaf. I may just have my first victim! I park my scooter right in front of the glass door just as he is turning the sign to "Closed."

"Wait, Mr. Gaines," I yell, rapping on the door. It takes him several tries, but he finally retracts the slide on the bolt.

He's a tiny man, maybe five foot six at the most. His scalp has only the occasional tuft of gray hair, and he looks like he's fighting the mange as opposed to male pattern baldness. Not a tooth in his head, glasses about an inch and half thick, and ear canals so twined with wiry hairs that a gnat can't squeeze through, surely I'd be doing Mr. Gaines a favor by taking him out.

"I have. The stuff. Your mom. Asked for.

Behind. The counter, Iris," he says through pursed lips in between raggedy breaths.

"It's not Iris; it's Magnolia." He doesn't hear me and continues to shuffle towards the counter. I take in the sight around me: row after row of canvases, paints, paint brushes, easels, and arts and crafts supplies. I spy a case of hobby knives, and suddenly, a plan unfolds. Knife to the neck should be quick and easy. I nervously chew on my thumbnail for a second before palming the largest instrument I can find and hiding it behind my back. The shuffling continues for what seems like an eternity, and my heart pounds faster and harder with each step. As soon as he makes it through the bar flap, I'll pounce!

"I'm sorry I have to do this to you, Mr. Gaines, but you'll forever be known as the Red Daisy's first victim. Therefore, your death will not be in vain," I mumble as I stealthily shadow him, hobby knife poised and ready to sink into his flesh.

"Did. You..." He spins around, and because I'm so close to him, he actually walks into the blade. A steady flow a dark red blood pours from the small incision in his neck. He quickly raises his hand to cover the wound, and his eyebrows arch upwards from curiosity as he pulls away his hand to eye the crimson fluid all over it. "Well. I'll. Be."

I didn't get to hear what he said after that. An uncomfortable pressure on my sternum draws me from the darkness, and it's not until I struggle to open my eyes that I feel a sudden rush of intense pain throughout my entire face. I try to draw my hand to it, but it won't work yet.

"Begonia, can you hear me? Wake up for me."

"If. She. Doesn't. Answer. To. That, then. Pick. Another. Flower. Her. Name. Is. A. Flower."

"Lily? Chrysanthemum? I don't really know a lot of flower names," a masculine voice says from above.

"Hurtshhhhh," I say with a whistle. *Why am I whistling?* I run my tongue over my teeth. *Oh shit! They aren't there!* I suddenly become aware of the coppery, metallic taste in my mouth. *Oh, my God! My teeth are GONE! I have no front teeth!* The sudden adrenaline surge compels me to run away, but I'm held fast by strong hands.

"Don't move, okay? My name is Jace Taylor, and I'm a paramedic. You're in good hands. Just try to relax, and I'll explain everything to you. You're okay. I know you're in pain, but you're going to be just fine." His voice is velvety smooth and so hypnotic that my muscles follow his command and unclench. The most seductive pair of blue eyes stare into mine once I'm able to keep my lids open. I'm completely and utterly speechless.

"Hi," he says with a smile. "Welcome back. What's your name, sweetheart?"

I feel my face flush. No one has ever called me sweetheart, well, no one besides Sunny or Big Daddy. "Mach. Machhhh." My lips refuse to cooperate!

"Shhh. It's okay. Do you have a driver's license or something with your name on it in your bag?"

I will DIE if he opens my bag! I need to quit carrying so many inappropriate and embarrassing things in my purse! I shake my head, and he says, "That's okay. We're going to get you to the hospital now." I give a nervous nod, unsure of what to expect. Jace and his partner shift me to a stretcher, and once I feel it starting to roll, I reach up to feel my face. Everything is foreign. My nose is three times its normal size and shifted to the right. One cheek protrudes about an inch higher than the other, and I'm not even sure if I have lips anymore; they just kind of flow into the swollen cheek.

"Try not to get upset. I know it feels off right now, but you'll be amazed what miracles a good doctor and a little time can make. Try to relax, ma'am."

Ma'am? How old does he think I am? I study his features to see if I can guess his age. Short, dark blond hair. Clean shaven. Crystal blue eyes. Slight wrinkling around the corner of his eyes. A body that suggests a lot of his free time is spent at the gym. He has an older, yet playful air about him. I guess he's in his mid-thirties?

The stretcher is locked into place in the back of the ambulance, and Jace tosses my messenger bag between my calves before taking a seat opposite me. He checks my blood pressure, shines a light into my eyes, and lifts his eyebrows as his takes my pulse.

"Still nervous?" he asks. He has no clue that he's the first man to ever lay hands on me for longer than a second. His touch ignites something deep inside, especially when his fingers leave my wrist and begin to palpate various areas of my body.

"Does this hurt? Is it sore?" he asks, running his hand over my collarbones. I shake my head. My body is on fire! "What about here?" he asks, his hands on either side of my rib cage. If I had teeth and a lip that wasn't the size of a sausage, I'd bite it. "Anything here?" he questions, gripping my hips and giving them a slight squeeze. My breathing quickens. Wait! He's moving down the length of my body! I don't shave my legs! Haven't done it in three years! He's going to find a freaking forest! I bet he'll puke. A million thoughts plague my mind at once. *Get him back up here! Get him back up here! Make him abort! Cough! Wheeze! Do something!*

A mixture of a sneeze, cough, snort, and laugh spews forth, and Jace is instantly at my side. "Are you feeling sick? You swallowed some blood and that irritates the stomach. Do you feel like you're going to vomit?" I shake my head as tears seep from the corners of my eyes. That damned distraction hurt like hell!

He gently strokes my hair. "I'm sorry. I know it hurts. We're almost to the hospital. How about we play a game? I'm going to try to guess your name. Mr. Gaines told me that it's a flower name. I'm going to run through the alphabet, and when I hit the first letter of your name, you squeeze my hand. Okay?" he asks, sliding his hand into mine. I want to swoon. "A. B. C...." When he gets to *M*, I give a squeeze. "Okay, flowers that start with an M. Marigold? Mimosa? Wait, is that a drink or a flower?" he asks. I don't care. The longer he takes to guess, the longer he holds my hand! "Magnolia?" Darn! I give his hand a squeeze.

He reclines back comfortably against the backrest of his seat. "Magnolia. That's a new one, and believe me, I come across some pretty unique names in this business." All I can do is give a semi-gurgle as I reply. "Here, let me help you. This is just like the spit sucker at the dentist, just bigger." He places the long, rigid catheter into the corner of my mouth, and I no longer feel as though I'm drowning. "Better, right? I can see it in your eyes," he says. "Here, you hold it, and use it whenever you feel. We're about two blocks from the hospital, 'k?"

I sort of roll my eyes a bit in place of a verbal "yes." The ambulance stops, and though my face is killing me, I'm a little sad that the ride is over. Jace would soon be a memory, and goodness only knows what tortures await me beyond those sliding glass doors! I take a mental photograph of Jace's firm, tight ass as he bends his tall frame to exit the back of the ambulance. He wooshes by me quickly, so I wasn't afforded much of a gaze. Damn! My libido suddenly bottoms out when I see the reaction of bystanders as I'm rolled down the hallway.

Full grown men suddenly turn pale when they see me, a woman gasps, and behind me I hear heaving. Oh, my God! How bad is my face? I desperately try to turn my head in search of Jace, who I know is at the head of the stretcher. He puts his hand on my shoulder. "Relax; you're okay." Some of the tension leaves when I feel his touch.

"Hi, Jace," a very soft spoken bleached blonde says coming from behind the nurses' station. "She goes to room five." She holds up five fingers while coyly twisting her ponytail with her fingers.

"Five it is, Nancy. Catch you on the way out?" Jace asks.

"Maybe," she flirtatiously replies. She gives him a quick wink before swiping a clipboard from a rack on the desk and disappearing down the hall. We enter the room the nurse has assigned, and Jace and his partner help me get from their stretcher to the hospital's. A male nurse and female doctor enter before the transfer is complete.

"Big J!" the burly male nurse calls.

"You know it," Jace says tapping elbows with the man. "And the ravishing Dr. Cloudia James as treating physician—nice. You're in good hands, Maggie."

"It's Claudia, not Cloudia," she says, taking my hand lightly in hers. "Private joke," she says as an aside. "Give me details about this case."

Casually propping his forearms on the vacated stretcher, Jace begins, "According to Mr. Gaines, the owner of the art shop, Magnolia, our patient here," he says, nodding in my direction, "was trying to buy a hobby knife. Mr. Gaines is nearly blind and hard of hearing, so he didn't realize she was right behind him. He turned, startling her, and she nicked his neck. There was blood, and syncope followed. Ms. Last-Name-Still-Undetermined," he winks at me, "collapsed. She did a nosedive into the counter then wound up face down on the tile floor. Most of her teeth are missing; we managed to salvage some." He holds up a plastic specimen cup that looks like Chiclets floating in pale pink water. "Vitals were stable on scene and remained so en route."

Dr. James palpates the more tender areas of my face. "I'm sorry. I know it hurts." She shines a light in my eyes, up my nose, and into my mouth, and then orders a series of tests. Mack, the burly male nurse, scribbles some notes onto the chart while Jace and Dr. James huddle in the corner.

I'm nervous they're discussing something about my condition, but it's clear from their body language that the conversation is entirely personal. They step out the room, and I'm left alone with Big Mack. He's huge and bald, except for a little ring that starts about an inch above his ears, and intimidating as hell. His skin is the color of dark chocolate, and his eyes, rich amber. He looks more like a professional wrestler than a nurse.

"Hello? Can you hear me?" Mack snaps his fingers near my ear. I nod. "Okay, thought you zoned out on me for a minute. Do you have an ID on you?" I shake my head. "In here?" he asks, dangling my bag from the tip of one of his sausage-like fingers. I'm mesmerized by his swinging jowls. It's hypnotic. Back and forth, back and forth they swing with each word he says. There are two, then four, back to two. *Why won't my eyes focus?* "The drugs must be kicking in. Doc gave you some pain medication in your IV."

When did I get an IV? How long have I been here? Jowls. I laugh to myself. *That's a funny word. Jow-els. Jow-ellls. Jow...* I'm out.

three

I'm on a deserted island. A sultry breeze does nothing to stop the beads of sweat from pooling into the bra of my makeshift bikini top. I toss down the pestle in my hand to wipe my dripping brow, and as I reach to pick it up, I spy Jace making his way down the beach with a string of fish. He's nude, except for the tiniest scrap of fabric that winds around his hips— tight, toned, and all man. My heart thuds in response to the very sight of him.

"Mags, why would you do this to yourself? Look at you, all hot and sweaty. You know that I like to handle all of the physical work. You may lounge, frolic, swim, anything your heart desires, but all work should be left to me."

"I'm sorry. I forgot," I say with a pout.

"Your insubordination calls for punishment. Wait here for me." He's gone for only a minute or so before returning with a hollowed out coconut filled with cool water. "Drink. It's important for you to

stay hydrated." I drink the majority of it, but some of it streams down my throat and chest. "We must not waste precious fluids." Jace dips his head low, his tongue eagerly lapping the salty water from my chest. My nerve endings ignite. He pulls off my top to continue licking around and under my breasts, then plants small, tender kisses all the way down to my navel.

"Take off your skirt," he orders. Without batting an eye, I do so. He sits on the trunk of a low slung coconut tree, then motions that I should lie across his lap. His hand makes contact with my bare bottom, and I bite my lip to stop the pleasure-filled scream from escaping. Again and again, he taps my ass with his palm. I'm oblivious to everything but the feel of his firm hand and his growing erection pressing hard against my belly. He stops what he's doing to carefully place me on the sand. "I hope I wasn't too hard on you." His eyes look deeply into mine. "That was just part one of your punishment. Part two begins now."

"Part two?" I ask coyly. "What are you going to do to me?"

"I'm going to fill you with my nine inch penis, over and over again, until you beg for mercy. I know it's harsh, but..."

"No buts. You're right," I quickly say. He lowers his head to kiss me. He grows closer and closer until I feel his lips on mine. My fingers gingerly run through his... Wait. Jace's hair is short.

What I'm feeling is long and fluffy. My eyes fly open, and if my jaw weren't wired shut, I'd be screaming bloody murder.

The golden retriever, who was now licking my hand, parks its rear onto the floor. The dog's owner, a gray-haired woman in her mid-sixties, looks down on me with a mixture of disbelief and disdain. *Oh, shit! My dream! What did I say? Nothing. I can't really talk right now. Uh, oh! I must've done something inappropriate. Shit! Shit! Shit!*

"We'll be moving to the next patient. Come, Scooter. Now!" The dog was instantly at her side. "Feel better soon," she tosses as an afterthought before shutting the door.

Almost as soon as the latch clicks into place, the cacophony starts. Big Daddy and Sunny arrive. She's in a muumuu, and nothing more, not even shoes. Her hair is braided loosely and wound into little circles on either side of her head. He's in his usual seersucker suit. The only thing different is that his long gray hair isn't neatly slicked back like it usually is; instead it's slightly disheveled and free from product.

"I'm utterly outraged! What an abomination! What a complete travesty this supposed healing facility is trying to pass off as modern medicine. I've just returned from the business office. Do you have any idea what they estimate this stay will cost? Highway robbery!" He begins to look around the room, gathering items into his arms. "Facial tissues, not a necessity. Did you drink from this mug? Of course not, your jaw is wired shut. It's going back!"

"Shorry, Shig Shatty," I manage to hiss. He sure didn't complain about money when he was forking it out for Sunny's new boobs. I roll my eyes.

"No, no, no, no! You have nothing to apologize for," Sunny says, taking the collection from Big Daddy's arms. "If anyone owes an apology, it's me. Those art supplies could've waited. Are you in much pain, Magnolia?"

I shrug. "Shwhat did shey do to me?"

"They pretty much reconstructed your face from the nose down," Sunny answers.

"Shwat! Shreconstucted my fash!"

"Now, now. Nothing to get upset about. The nasal splint will come off in about a week, and after your jaw heals, we'll see a specialist about your missing teeth." Sunny tugs on the string to open the blinds; the room is instantly flooded with sunshine. Squinting hurts, and it hurts bad! Once I start to whimper, she lowers them to something less blinding then takes a seat next to me. "Murray, take a walk."

He grumbles for a bit, but nonetheless, disappears from the room. "Are you feeling okay?" she asks, taking my frail hand in hers. I shrug. "You've been through a terrible ordeal. Don't listen to your father. He's upset because he won't get to play the heartbroken father who is desperate for justice because of the agony his poor disfigured daughter has suffered. I forbade him to even think of a lawsuit against Mr. Gaines. He's angry with me, not you."

I give a slight nod.

"Although, I don't understand what you were doing with a hobby knife. I didn't ask for one of those."

"Shrowject. Artsh and crasht. Shurprise."

"Oh, how lovely. Your artistic gene has finally kicked in! Shall I save you a spot in class? We're doing sailboats next week."

Remembering saggy balls and droopy boobs, I quickly decline by shaking my head, which I do a little too vehemently. The room starts to spin.

"That's okay, some other time," Sunny says, giving me a slight kiss on the forehead. "Your hair looks nice down and free flowing like this. It's been a long time since I've seen it in anything other than a bun. It's lovely. We'll see you later." After a soft pat on the head, she leaves the room. That's how Sunny and Big Daddy do things.

Curious as to how much damage my face had sustained, I reach over to the rolling table to my right and pull it close to me. Inside is a pop up mirror. I gasp when I see the face staring back at me. My swollen face is every shade of purple in the color spectrum. The thick white nasal splint only serves to draw more attention to how discolored my face truly is. My lips are double their normal size, and when I manage to pull them back some, all I see is a dark abyss. Disheartened, I try to get as much sleep as possible in between the blood pressure checks, the blood draws, the doctors' rounds, the food deliveries (which are pointless since I can't eat anything), and the medication administration. It turns out to be very little rest for me.

The next morning, Sunny and Big Daddy come back to the hospital because I'm being discharged. Everything is pretty much a repeat of the previous day, Big Daddy in his suit grumbling, Sunny in her revealing silky muumuu discussing sailboat painting, and me desperate to be anywhere but where I am. The discharge paperwork is signed, and a wheelchair is brought to the room. I'm free to go, and I can't wait to hide out in my apartment.

Big Daddy has control of the wheelchair, while Sunny walks behind us with my bag straps criss-crossed over her chest. She is either oblivious or totally enjoys the stares her getup is attracting.

We cross the threshold of the sliding glass doors, and the first thing I notice once we get outside is the ambulance in the bay. My eyes quickly dart around, half- hoping to see Jace, and half-hoping *not* to see Jace.

"Hey, Mags! They're sending you home?" his voice calls from nearby. My stomach flips. The brilliance of his bright white smile is overshadowed by his striking, crystal blue eyes.

"I don't remember naming my child Mags, young man. If I wanted her to be called Mags, I'd have named her such. Her name is Magnolia, and she should be referred to by said name."

"Hey, aren't you the guy on TV? You get people

money faster than grass through a goose or something like that?"

"I am, and if you can't tell, I'm trying to get my daughter home. Unless... Have you suffered a personal injury? Know someone who has?"

Jace shakes his head.

"Murray, leave him alone!" Sunny yells, bursting into a full-on jog. What Big Daddy did left me red, though no one can tell through all of the purple. However, what Sunny is doing, well, ...that makes me want to roll myself down the ER ramp and into oncoming traffic. It is as if everything is in slow motion. As she dashes towards us, one of Sunny's hands goes up while the opposite boob goes with it, then it jiggles wildly as her foot connects with the ground. It looks like two cantaloupes spiraling toward and then bouncing off each other. "Murray, I said to stop!" she says, finally catching up to us. Yep, I want to die, but all I can do is hang my head low. Damn the ground for not swallowing me up!

"I apologize for the name mix up. I'm glad you're doing better. Heal fast, Magnolia."

"Shank you." I'm pretty sure I spray him with spittle. I close my eyes and pray for a complete do-over. He lightly taps my shoulder. I know it's him because I feel the zing, which to my pleasure, is happening quite often. I think back to my dream from the day before, and I can't help but wonder how off those penile calculations are. When I open my eyes, his crotch is the first thing I see. I start to choke.

Jace squats in front of me. "Coughing is okay. I know it's a scary sensation, especially with your jaw wired shut. But, we don't start to worry until you can't make any noise. Go ahead. I'll stay here with you until you stop."

My eyes water, I'm pretty sure I rupture something in my nasal cavity, and I make some of the oddest noises ever emitted from a human, but I finally stop coughing. My gaze drifts to Jace's crotch again. *Damn it! Get a grip, woman!* The worst part is that I think he notices because he quickly bounces on his heels to stand upright, says a quick goodbye, and rejoins his partner at the ambulance. I'm humiliated!

"Let's get you home," Sunny says.

"Yesh! Pwease!" I say, utterly embarrassed, yet strangely turned on.

four

The first week home proves to be incredibly boring. I sleep for the most part, which is easy to do since I haven't had anything solid to eat since before the accident. When I'm not sleeping, I find myself pondering my quest for notoriety. Two things are for sure: I need to find a technique that doesn't involve blood, and I need to start working out because things that don't involve blood generally require brute strength. I feel queasy remembering the blood pouring from the small cut on Mr. Gaine's neck. Nope. Not gonna happen.

Is becoming a serial killer the only way I can make a name for myself? Men don't give me a second look, women ignore me, my parents tolerate me, and I have no discernible talent to speak of, so realistically, what other avenue do I have? I'll never be famous; infamy is definitely the best route. But, no blood. What do I do? Fire?

Arson requires hardly any physical strength, it's

virtually foolproof, and the necessary tools can be easily obtained. I can still be known as the Red Daisy. Instead of drawing on my victims, I'll draw my signature mark on an object near the structure. Genius! No mess on my part at all!

I suddenly feel a slight burst of energy and reach for my laptop to search accelerants, but I close it quickly. Who will be my first victim now? Mr. Gaines has well but earned his reprieve. One of the bad things about having no social life is that I know no one. Kind of makes it hard to pick a victim. Forlornly, I realize that my only option is to socialize. I'll have to partake in Sunny's class. Surely, one of the old coots in there will be teetering on death's door. I'll be doing him or her a favor! Oh, but at what cost? Sunny has a strict "nude only" policy for her art classes. How badly do I really want this? Pretty damned bad.

Donning a terrycloth robe, I anxiously peep through the glass windows of the in-house art studio. Sunny is stretching, which is downright disturbing from my angle. I lightly rap on the glass to garner her attention. At first she looks confused, then slightly perturbed, and finally, she hides it all with a smile.

"Is everything okay, Magnolia?" she asks, opening the glass door just wide enough to squeeze the words out.

"Shy wash hoping to take shore cwass today."

"Really? You want to take my class? Well, okay then! Welcome. The others should be arriving any moment. I know you don't have supplies, so pick a canvas from the shelf, and I'll put together a few things for you to use. We're going to be painting people frolicking in the park. Isn't that exciting?"

"Sure. Shounds gwate." Frustrated with my speech, I shake my head.

Sunny carries an assortment of acrylic paint tubes over to me. "Don't let negative thoughts and emotions mar today. You get all of your hardware removed in a week. Not too much longer now. Let's cleanse you of this negativity. Close your eyes, deep breath in…"

"I can't," I say, touching my nasal splint.

"Oh, well, never mind. Mr. Davis and Mr. Curtis are coming up the walk. They always take a spot in the front. You may set up wherever you like." She dashes to the door. "Hello, gentlemen! How are you this fine morning? Ready to create a masterpiece?" she sing songs.

"Hiya, Sunny! You're looking just as firm as ever," the older white man I know to be Mr. Davis says as he shuffles in the door. He drops his supplies on a nearby table and starts to unbutton his long sleeved dress shirt.

"Hey, I ain't even got in the door yet. Move yourself," Mr. Curtis, an octogenarian with cataracts so thick that his brown eyes are rimmed milky blue, says while pushing Mr. Davis aside.

"Ain't no need for shoving, Curtis. Lord knows why you're taking this class anyway. You're blind as a bat, you old fool."

"I see what counts. Plus, Sunny says painting is good therapy. Don't matter none that my paintings come out the way they do, it's just important that I try. Ain't that right, Sunny?"

"That's very right, Mr. Curtis. Come, let me share some of my positive energy with you." She takes the old man's dark, wrinkled hand into hers and pulls him in for a hug. A smile made broader due to his upper dentures being too big for his mouth erupts across his face, and Mr. Davis, a short, stocky bald man in his late seventies turns green with envy. He stomps off to claim the easel set directly in front of Sunny's station, stops to give me a quick onceover, shakes his head, then continues to set up his supplies in his original location. *Great! I can't even get a second glance from a seventy-something year old pervert.* I cinch my robe tighter.

Sunny helps Mr. Curtis to his easel, and I hear him telling Mr. Davis something about not being able to see, but he sure can feel just fine. Some heated words are exchanged between the two of them, but Ms. Agnes and Ms. Lola Mae show up, so the bickering stops. Obviously sweet on the old men, they giggle like school girls as they set up on either side of Mr. Davis and Mr. Curtis.

A few minutes later, more pupils come up the walkway, and the classroom looks like a haven for nursing home escapees—all except for one last minute straggler. He is young, like early twenties young, with puffy cheeks that look like they should be on a hoarding chipmunk. His brown hair is heavily oiled and parted to the left, while his beady little eyes are set so close together that I wonder if it's possible for him to see past his nose. He waddles in, claiming a spot near the door, and I'm curious as to what the strange sound is that I'm suddenly hearing. As he sets up his supplies, I realize the noise is coming from him. Wakeful snoring would be the best descriptor of the rumbling coming from the area.

Sunny presses a button and the melodious sound of a pan flute wafts through the air. Some might find it relaxing; all I can think of is Ralph Macchio and his karate movies. She encourages everyone to disrobe, giving her spiel about nudity increasing creativity because it puts us in touch with Mother Earth's energies and such. I only half listen because I'm devastated by the train wreck happening around me. As I watch the people disrobe, a few things become clear: Depends undergarments should sponsor this event, gravity is a friend to no one, and the hair old men lose from the top of their heads isn't really gone, it just multiplies and retreats to other body parts.

The only thing more disturbing than watching the cast from *Cocoon* disrobe is watching the late arrival undress. He pulls his oversized golf shirt over his head, and sets it on the table beside him. An undershirt, that I suspect was originally white but is now ear wax yellow, is the next to come off. My stomach turns when his movement causes one of the larger pimples from his back acne to shoot a load of pus towards Ms. Lola Mae. Both of them seem unfazed by the event. He unbuckles his belt, and the brown polyester slacks he's wearing practically launch themselves from his body. All that's left between him and the atmosphere is one pair of underwear that looks five sizes too small. Roll after roll of pasty white flesh gleams with sweat, though the temperature in the room is seventy degrees at most. He bends over to pull a handkerchief from his pant pocket, and I'm greeted by a muddy streak down the back of his drawers.

Bile and stomach acid rise in my throat desperately seeking escape. I begin to panic. My jaw is wired shut! My nose is still healing! What will happen if I puke? Stumbling around the room, I grasp onto the closest easel to me, but it falls over and smashes to the ground. Then goes another, and another. Like dominos, *boom, boom, boom, boom*, stand after stand falls over. The ruckus startles Ms. Agnes, who takes a tumble from her stool onto the floor. Making a last ditch effort to catch herself, she desperately grasps for anything to grab hold of. Unfortunately, that would be Mr. Davis' arm. He's forced to the ground with her, and together, they cry out in pain.

The commotion helps to alleviate my urge to purge, but the fact remains that two victims lie in agony on the cold tile floor. Skidmark pulls out his phone and dials 911, while Sunny and the rest of the group hover around the injured pair. Gasps, sobs, and curses fly through the room. Sunny does her best to bring calm to the room by offering cleansing chants. It's not working.

Hiding in the corner, I look with horror at the devastation I've caused. Skidmark notices and begins to make his way towards me. He smells like old bacon grease and moth balls. My stomach tries to revolt again, but I'm able to quash it.

"You look upset. I can comfort you, if you'd let me," he confidently says with a smirk.

"No, shanks," I say, rapidly shaking my head.

He props his arm against one of Sunny's bookshelves, and all I can focus on are the little balls of fabric hanging from his pit hair like tiny ornaments on a bushy, smelly tree. He must assume that I'm drawn to his physique because he straightens up to puff out his chest. "I try to hit the gym at least one, two times a year. You look toned. Do you work out, too?"

Again, I shake my head.

"My name's Jefferson, but my friends call me Diablo because I like to ride, and I'm kinda wild, so you should probably beware," he says to me as though he's letting me in on a huge secret. His breath smells like raw onions. My nose twitches in response. He runs his hand down his doughy chest. "It's okay if you feel drawn to me. I know how you women like bad boys. I'm single at the moment, but I can't guarantee that will last long. The list of brokenhearted maidens I've left in my dust is long, but I have a feeling that we can have something special, girl. What do you say? Can you handle Diablo?" he breathes.

Boyfriend? I've never in my entire life had a man I could call by that title, and even though his very being repulses the hell out of me, I fall in love with the idea of having a real relationship to call my own. Maybe I would finally have a first date! Better late than never, right?

"Okay, I'll be your girfwiend," I say.

"Right on, baby. Diablo's gonna take care of his woman. What's your name?"

"Magnolia," I manage to say through the wires.

"Yeah, you need a new name. I'm gonna call you Mindy, okay?"

"But, my name shish Magnolia," I insist.

"Yeah, baby, but you look like a Mindy to me."

I shrug. The glare from the windshield of the ambulance as it turns into the driveway pulls me back to the issue at hand, the injured pupils. My heart pitter pats when I spy Jace and his partner walking toward the classroom. He enters the room with all the confidence of a super hero.

"Hi, I'm Jace. I hear someone's had an accident, and I'm here to help. Whoa! What do we have here?" he asks, taking a slight step back when he realizes that he's in a room full of elderly naked people.

Sunny rises and extends her hand to him. "This is

my art class."

"Wait, I remember you from somewhere…" he thinks about it for a few seconds. "Of course! Magnolia's mom." It didn't seem to faze him that he was speaking to a nude woman. "Okay, let's make some room people. Let me get in there." He squeezes past some of the bystanders crowding around the fallen two. "I understand that you're concerned for your friends, but the best thing you can do is to step back and give us room to work, please. Right over there, against the wall would be best. Thank you."

The group begins to shuffle in the direction he suggests. As they move away, Jace glances around the room, and his eyes land on me. Well, not just me, but Diablo, too. His arm is possessively draped over my shoulder, and I feel as though I might collapse from his weight. Not to mention the fact that my nose is burning from the odors creeping into my inflamed passages. Jace gives a slight smile, then goes about his business.

Once the patients are packaged up and ready to be transported, Jace comes in to do one last search for any left behind equipment or supplies. "Looks like you're healing well, Maggie. Sorry, Magnolia."

"What's it to you, jerk face?" Diablo asks, removing his arm from around my neck, and jutting his pimply jaw forward.

"Down, boy. I was just checking to see how she was feeling since her accident, is all. This your boyfriend?" he asks, his finger lining up with Diablo's bloated belly. I wonder if he'll laugh like the dough boy if Jace touches him.

"I shink sho," I reply with a mixture of embarrassment and insecurity. Jace's face shows uncertainty as he gives a sort of half nod our way.

"Okay then. Well, you take care now," he says, walking towards the door.

"That's right. She's Diablo's woman now. Feel the burn! Oh, yeah," he says while making shooing motions at Jace. I stare ahead blankly, wondering if having a boyfriend is worth all of this. Jace leaves, and while Diablo is getting dressed, I catch sight of the massive skid mark again. After a full body shiver, I cinch my robe more tightly around my body.

"Come on, Mindy. I'll let you buy me a sandwich," he says once he finishes sliding on his loafers. "Mindy," he yells, snapping his fingers. I'm pulled from my trance.

"Shorry, I don't shink I want a boyfwend anymore."

"What? You want me to buy you a sandwich? Cause I can do that."

"No. No shanks," I say. He falls to his knees, and quickly shuffles my way. Melodramatic sobs wrack his body.

"Please, please, please don't break up with me. I've never had a girlfriend before, I mean, not a real one. Please! I'll do anything. Just stick around long enough for one of my friends to see you. The guys won't believe me if I tell them. They'll want proof."

He hugs my ankles, and I remember the ten inch long leg hairs I'm sporting.

"Fine! Get up! I'll be your girffriend fer one week, but zat's it."

"Deal." He stops sniveling and rises to his feet. "May I take you to dinner tonight, Magnolia?"

"I thought you shed I looked like a Mindy."

"Magnolia's your name. I'll just call you that."

"Okay."

"You get to pick the place: McDonald's? Burger King? No. Tonight is special. I wouldn't normally do this, but tonight we'll go ethnic and eat at Taco Bell. You don't even have to order from the value menu." He pulls out a small wad of money and quickly counts it. "Anything you want. As long as it's not more than six dollars, it's yours!" He puts his arm around me again, and he guides me towards the exit. "When and where do I pick you up?"

"Here. I live here. I can't eat, but you can pick me up whenever," I answer.

"You live here? Sunny's your mom? No shit! You're kidding me, right?"

"No," I answer.

"Damn, what happened to you? Was your dad beaten with an ugly stick or something?"

If I didn't have so much hardware in and on my face, he would've seen my jaw drop, followed by an angry flare of the nostrils. Instead, he gets my palm against his robust cheek without the rest of the hoopla. His beady eyes narrow, and he starts to breathe quickly through his nose. "You hit me!" he fusses, his voice laden with fury.

"No shit," I say, stomping up the stairs to get to my apartment.

"Wait! Wait! What I said was probably not the most appropriate thing to say. Give me another chance to make it up to you. Please!" He joins me on the landing at the top of the stairs. There isn't much room up there, and his close proximity makes me more nervous than normal. "Let me make it up to you."

I have nowhere to run as his wide body pins mine against the door. He pushes his large mitt of a hand against my forehead to angle my head back, and then he begins to hurriedly lick at my lips with his tongue like a dog lapping water from a bowl. I'd never experienced a kiss other than the very rare chaste one with Sunny or Big Daddy, so I have no idea if what he's doing to me is the norm. Something inside tells me that it might not be. I turn my head away, repulsed by the sensation and the nasty taste.

"You go! Go now!" I say as loudly as possible.

"Was that not right? Did I do that wrong? I've only kissed Sasha, and she seemed to like it."

"Ish Sasha your dog?" I ask, rubbing my lips with the back of my sleeve.

"No!" His voice cracks as he yells the reply defensively.

I give him a blank stare. "She's more than a dog. Don't judge! Leave me alone! Don't ever talk to me again!" He takes the first eight steps as quickly as his legs will carry him, and the next eight, he takes on his ass as he bounces down each one individually. He jumps back up when he hits the ground and makes a mad dash towards his moped. He's still doing a mumble/wail thing as the motor sputters to life. The moped loses about four inches of height when he sits on it, and the engine pleads for mercy when he hammers on the gas. Well, I can finally say I've had a boyfriend. It only lasted about twenty minutes, but that's a start, right?

five

I've been spending a lot of time staring in the mirror since the procedures to my face were completed. My nose is no longer beak-like; it is cute with the slightest upturn to it. My new teeth are pearly white and straight as can be. I smile broadly. Not a trace of the bucktoothed mess that used to fill my mouth.

As soon as the wires came off, all I did was inhale food. I couldn't seem to get full, and my figure is now showing it. I have a slight tummy pooch, something I've never had, and my face looks fuller and rosier. The cups of my bra can't contain the spill over, and I have hips! I practice a new way of walking to show off my new assets. It's far from graceful, but maybe one day I'll get it down. Despite the changes, I'm still an unrecognized plain Jane, so my master plan must move forward. After some research on the internet and a quick trip to the hardware store, I'm ready to delve into the world of arson.

I wait for one of Sunny and Big Daddy's weekends away before I begin. According to the myth debunkers, pig is the closest to human flesh, so I order a quarter of a pig from Mr. Landry, the butcher, and he tells me he'll have it ready for me in an hour. I hop on the Vespa, give the front basket a good wiggle to make sure it's attached firmly, and then take off for the butcher shop. True to his word, it's waiting for me. Problem is, a quarter of a pig is not small, and there is no way it will *ever* fit into my dinky basket.

"Well, Magnolia, what did you expect?" Mr. Landry, gruffly questions. He's an older man who dyes his hair jet black to match his bushy mustache. His attire is always a blood stained white t-shirt, blue jeans with a bandana hanging out of the pocket, and white rubber boots. He keeps a cigarette tucked behind his ear, though I know for a fact that he quit smoking two years ago. Mr. Landry is not very nice, but he's the closest meat man around.

"Uh, I guess like a ham or something."

"No!" he yells, smacking his knife onto the butcher block. "If you want a ham, you order a ham! You do not order a quarter of a pig!"

I do a sort of apologetic cringe before speaking again. "But, how will I get this home?" I ask, staring wide-eyed at the long, paper-wrapped package.

"Not my problem! You can ride it home for all I care!"

I struggle to pull it off the counter top, and right then and there, I vow to start working out with weights. Swaying from side to side while lugging it out the door, I finally manage to get the hunk of pig into the parking lot. I sigh heavily after plopping it onto the seat of the Vespa. There's no way it's going into the basket. Desperate for ideas, I look around the deserted parking lot for an answer. With no other options presenting themselves, I decide to take Mr. Landry's advice, and I straddle the thickest portion of the package. I'm going to ride the pig leg home.

I have quite a few near misses on the way home, the latter of which causes full-on brake squealing and tire screeching from the red sports car trying to pass me. I wager a glimpse behind me, and to my dismay, the lower third of the pig's foot is now free from the wrapping. I look like a witch flying a pig's leg, but I'm too close to home to pull over.

I park the Vespa as close to the garage door as possible, and the pig leg clunks to the ground when I dismount. Rolling my eyes with disgust, I plop a seat on the thickest portion of the pig hind quarter, and with my chin in my palm, I debate my next course of action. It doesn't take me long to figure out that my two options are to leave it or to use brute force. Thus begins the game of tug of war with Porky. Taking the hoof end in my grip, I drag the carcass a foot or two then I rest for a while. This stop/start inch fest continues until I finally get the hunk of meat to the backyard and into the fire pit. Sincerely wanting to keep my vow to get some muscles, I promise to start using Sunny's home gym tomorrow.

After taking a few minutes to catch my breath, I survey the line of chemicals before me. Randomly picking two, simply because I liked their labels, I pop the tops and begin to douse the pig. An intense flame burns brightly on the match stick I strike against the box, and as the flame dances and flickers at the end of it, I'm mesmerized. The heat finally registers in my fingertips, so I quickly toss it into the fire pit. Nothing happens. I light another one and toss it in. Nothing happens. Match after match is ignited and tossed into the smelly pit, and much to my frustration, the only thing I get in return is the tiniest puff of smoke.

"That's it. I give up. Evidently, arson isn't my thing eith…" *Whoosh!*

A fireball the size of Rhode Island engulfs me, but I manage to fall over backwards and crab crawl away from the intense heat. Coughing and hacking, I crawl to a spot under a magnolia tree and begin to assess bodily damage. Though my eyes are watering, I can see that my feet, legs, and skirt are all intact. Dirty, but not charred.

I never hear the sirens of the responding fire trucks. Maybe because I'm so preoccupied with the whole head-on-fire thing? A ruckus ensues, and I'm doused with water, a wet sheet placed over my head, and I'm forced to lie down on the itchy grass. An oxygen mask covers my face, and I'm instructed to lie still. I think it's overkill, but my head is starting to throb some, so I do as the firefighter instructs.

A few minutes later, the edge of the sheet is lifted, and I'm staring into a familiar set of crystal blue eyes. "Magnolia? Want to explain what happened?" Jace asks, removing the oxygen mask from my face.

"I wanted to roast a pig," I answer.

"Expecting a crowd?" he plies.

"No."

He squints. "You intended to roast seventy pounds of pig for yourself?"

"When you say it like that, it does sound a bit much." What in the world am I supposed to tell him? I hate my life. I hate being invisible. I'm trying to figure out the best way to kill someone, so I can kill others and become one of the most famous serial killers ever. Yeah, that will go over really well! I have to stick to my "hungry for pig" story.

"You must have one hell of a craving for pig. And normally, people don't pour accelerant over the pig and then toss in a match. There's a little more to a cochon de lait than your method," he says, waving his partner away. "I got this, Joe." Joe happily strikes up a conversation with one of the firefighters.

"Yeah, I think I just figured that out," I say.

He carefully unravels the rest of the sheet from my head, and I'm not sure how to read his look. It's kind of a cross between concerned and amused. "I have good news and bad news," he says, crossing his arms over his chest then pinching his lower lip between his thumb and forefinger.

"Okay, what's the good news?" I ask.

"Your burns don't appear to be anything too serious."

"Bad news?"

"You've suffered some hair loss."

"Hair…loss?" My fingers drift upwards and land where my eyebrows used to be. Where in the hell are my eyebrows! Oh, my God! WHERE IS MY HAIR! There are so many questions I want to ask, but the words won't leave my throat.

"Hey, try to calm down, Mags. You still have some hair, and what's gone will grow back with time."

I pat around to assess the damage, and as near as I can tell, I look like Larry from the Three Stooges, bald on the top, and a ring of kinky, bushy hair around the rest. Heartbroken, I pull the oxygen mask back over my face and stare off into the darkening sky. Jace pulls the mask off me. "Hey, it's not so bad. There are wigs and stuff. Come on. Let's get you to the hospital so they can check you out."

"Do I have to go?" I ask.

"No, but I think it's best that you do," he answers, smiling a sexy sort of half grin. "Do you want me to call your boyfriend? What's his name? Demon or something? I can have him meet us at the emergency room if you'd like."

"Diablo. And thanks, but we broke up."

"Oh, I'm sorry if I caused any hurt feelings to resurface."

"Nah, we only dated for twenty minutes."

Jace throws his head back and laughs heartily. "Twenty minutes? That has to be a record. Okay, Mags. Ready to load up and go?"

"No, I really think I'd just like to go upstairs, take a shower, and go to bed. I'm fine. Not much is hurting except my pride." I slowly sit up, and Jace extends a hand to help me to my feet. A jolt of energy shoots from his hand and surges through my body. He gives me a few friendly pats on the back.

"You sure?"

"Yeah, I'm sure," I say, taking off towards the stairs. I couldn't care less that the backyard is still crawling with firemen. I figure they'll leave when they're ready.

"Magnolia, I have some paperwork that you have to sign saying I offered to bring you to the hospital, but you didn't want to go."

"Sure, okay. Bring it over," I mumble. He points out a few spots on a form, and I scribble my name accordingly.

He lifts an eyebrow at me. "Need help getting settled? I feel bad leaving you like this. You don't look so good."

"I feel fine. It's just a disappointing day is all."

"You must've really wanted to eat that roast pig to be this forlorn over it," he mentions.

"Yeah, something like that. Thanks for coming

out to check on me."

"Of course. If you start to feel bad, call, okay?"

"Okay," I agree. One together, two together... I start my stair climbing ritual, and once I'm at the top of the landing, I give Jace a little wave before entering the apartment. I disrobe, shower, and sit down at the vanity to assess the damage. It is so much worse than I thought: bald at the top, a mix between super short and long scraggly pieces everywhere else, no eyebrows. I try not to cry, but it doesn't work. I boo-hoo myself to sleep, partly over my hair, and partly over the fact that I'd failed again. I hope that a good night's sleep will make things seem a little better in the morning, or better yet, that this is all just a bad dream.

*****

My eyes are super puffy when I try to open them, but I can't let that stop me. Another unanticipated consequence to my little barbecue —the smell. Rotting pig carcass is quite odoriferous, and my parents will be returning from their jaunt within a day or so. I quickly tie a bandana around my semi-bald head, a la Aunt Jemima style, then head to the fire pit. The sight before me is about as bad as the smell. Maggots and flies crawl over the charred, putrefying meat. I want to hurl, but the sense of urgency to get rid of the carcass trumps it.

I disappear into the garage for a bit where I find a

clothespin for my nose, some rope, a pair of black dot gloves, and of course, my trusty sunshine yellow Vespa. Gnawing on my lower lip, I try to determine the best course of action. There is no way in hell that I'm straddling this pig now!

Even though I heave the entire time, I manage to lasso one end of the rope around the pig hoof with the other end secured around my waist. My plan is to hop on the Vespa and drag the chunk of pork to the bayou towards the back of the property. It was foolproof in my mind.

I ease on the gas, but nothing happens except for a slight tightening of the rope around my waist. No time for playing around; I have to get this done! I hammer down on the throttle. The Vespa careens forward; I, however, do not. The pain of smashing into the ground is instantaneous and intense. I quickly rub my sore ribs then survey my hand. No blood. After untying the rope from my waist, I dust off and very gently mount the Vespa. Once it's back in its usual spot in the garage, I desperately search for plan B.

The only thing that looks like it will even remotely be an option is the huge green tractor that Big Daddy occasionally uses to piddle around with lawn projects. Climbing aboard, I'm confused by all of the buttons and levers before me, and I thankfully find one clearly marked, "Start." I push it; nothing happens. I jostle a few levers, and in doing so, I finally spot a key. I turn it, and then push the "Start" button. The tractor roars to life and shoots out of the stall like green lightening. I'm barely able to hold on to the steering wheel as I struggle to stay in the seat. I press and mash anything and everything in front of me, but nothing slows down the tractor. I aim it toward the fire pit, hoping the sturdy brick will stop the tractor for me. It doesn't. It plows right through the brick, sending shards of mortar and baked clay everywhere. Once I'm through the dust cloud, I see that I'm dragging the pig with me, so I steer towards the bayou. With any luck, I can cut the wheel once I get close enough and slingshot that sucker into the water. As for the tractor, if I have to ride it in circles around the property until it runs out of gas, then so be it.

I feel like I'm playing a game of chicken. The water's edge rapidly approaches, and I know that I have to time it just right for my plan to work. As soon as the embankment starts to slope downhill, I cut the wheel sharply to the right, and I feel the tractor starting to tip over. I heave my body in the opposite direction of the overturning vehicle, flying through the air Supergirl-style. I land with thud, and once I'm able to breathe again, I quickly sit up to assess the damage. The tractor's top half is completely submerged in the muddy water. Bubbles and steam surround the wreckage, and all I can do is stare with disbelief. Big Daddy will kick me out for this one, for sure. I look to my left, and there sits the nasty, smelly pig quarter mocking me.

"You stupid, no good, pain in my ass! Go away!" I yell to the rotting meat. Kicking it feels really good until I suddenly feel myself levitate. Before my brain can process what's going on, I'm set back on the ground, and Jace is standing before me.

"What did that poor pig ever do to you?" he jokes. I don't answer because I'm still out of breath from my rage fest. He surveys the damage; his gaze fixes on the overturned tractor. "Want to talk about it?"

I shake my head.

"Are you hurt?" he asks.

I shrug.

"Can I help you?"

"I don't think anyone can help me," I say, holding back the sob that wants to come. It plants itself firmly in my throat as a gigantic lump.

"Mags, I don't really know you, but I can tell you this, if you want help, you have to be unafraid to ask for it. Would you like my help?"

"Jace, why are you here?"

"My partner is new, and he forgot a piece of equipment at one of our calls. I've been retracing our route, hoping to find it. You haven't seen an oxygen cylinder around here, have you?"

"I don't recall seeing one," I answer truthfully.

"Damn. Okay," he says with a sigh. "Thanks."

"Jace."

He's rubbing the back of his neck with his palm. "Yeah?" he asks, preoccupied.

"Do you really think you can help me fix this mess?" I ask.

"What? Oh, yeah. Of course. No problem." He pulls out his cell phone and places a call to a friend of his who owns a wrecker truck. "Lee will be here in about an hour or so. He's on a call, but he promises to head this way as soon as he finishes up."

"Thanks," I say, starting to feel a little more optimistic.

"No problem. Want to tell me what the pig leg is doing over here?" he asks.

"It stinks, so I was trying to toss it into the water."

"With the tractor?"

"No, at first, I used my scooter, but that didn't go so well." I lift my turtleneck to show my midriff, and Jace sucks in a breath.

"What is that from? Is that a rope burn?"

I nod, and he tries his best not to laugh. Slowly lowering my shirt, I turn to walk away from him. He touches my shoulder.

"Maggie, you had to know that wouldn't end well, right?"

I hold my hand out towards the sunken tractor. "I have a history of not thinking things through before acting upon my ideas."

"I can see that. Okay, hand me those gloves from over there, please." He puts on the black dot gloves, claps his hands together a couple of times, and then shrugs his shoulders to limber up. Squatting low, he lifts the remains and easily tosses them into the water. How it's possible to be turned on by watching a man lift rotting pig, I have no clue, but I'm hot with desire. He misreads my flushed skin, rapid breathing, and closed eyes as something entirely different. "Let me wash up, and I'll assess that wound better. Is it causing you much pain?"

It really isn't, but a living, breathing human being without colonies of acne and visible skidmarks is willing to help me! I'm all over it!

"Upstairs?" he asks, pointing towards my apartment. There is no way in hell that I'm letting him into my porn cave.

"No. The house, please," I say, opening the side door for him to walk through. We pass Sunny's art studio, and continue down the hallway until the house opens to a large kitchen/living room combo. Standing behind Jace, I take full advantage of his preoccupation with soaping up to give him a thorough scan. His short, dark blond hair looks freshly shorn. In fact, all of the other times I'd seen him, he looked that way. He must be at the barber once a week. His tanned neck disappears beneath the collar of his dark button up shirt, and my gaze travels to his thick, broad shoulders. I want to run my hands over them so badly… to massage them, kiss them, playfully sink my teeth into them.

"You okay?" Jace asks, snapping me back to reality.

"Uh, yeah. Fine," I say, trying to hide my

embarrassment.

"Where can I throw this?" he asks, holding wadded up used paper towels.

"Oh, I'm sorry. Over there," I say, pointing to the cabinet door to his right. He tosses it, and with a slight chuckle, he asks to see my wound.

"It's not funny," I snap defensively.

"I'm sorry. You have to know that I try like hell to remain professional when it comes to medicine, but Mags, darling, it's very hard to do that with you."

"Are you saying that I'm the only accident-prone person you've ever encountered in your however many years of being a medic?"

"No way. Far from it. Let's just say that you're the most memorable."

"Really? I'm memorable? Is that a good thing or a bad thing?"

"I'm not sure," he says, nodding his head towards the sofa. "I'm thinking it's bad for you, since you generally wind up injured. The doctors did great job replacing your teeth and such."

"Yeah, Big Daddy is still bitching about that bill," I reply, taking a seat.

He looks thoughtful for a moment. "Your parents, they're pretty... I mean your mom teaches nude art lessons, and your dad is famous for his court theatrics. I'd imagine that life gets pretty hard for you sometimes. Almost like they overshadow your existence, right?"

At first I'm relieved because someone actually

understands where I'm coming from, but then I feel embarrassed. Who wants to admit that she's nothing, a complete nobody, in the eyes of everyone— including her parents?

"They're eccentric, but I know they love me," I answer, hoping he'll change the subject.

"I'm sure they do," he replies with a nod. "Is it okay if I raise your shirt to get a look at your abdomen?"

Lying back on the sofa, I agree. His fingers grip the hem of my turtleneck, slowly pulling it higher and higher until it rests just below my breasts. I'm instantly covered in goose bumps.

"Cold?" he asks, sitting beside me on the sofa. I nod, though these goose bumps don't have a damned thing to do with temperature. I try to keep my breathing calm and steady as his fingers trace the abrasion that mars the milky skin of my upper abdomen. "Any pain?"

"No, nothing serious. Just sore," I finally get out. He closes one eye and gives me a look that says, *Are you sure?* I nod.

"Okay. If anything changes, make sure you get checked out," he says, pulling my shirt back down.

"I will. Thank you," I say, rising to my feet. "Can I get you something to eat or drink?" I ask, desperate to come up with a reason to get him to stay a little longer.

"No thanks, I'm good. I need to find that missing cylinder. Lee should be here shortly, and he'll take care of that tractor situation."

I follow Jace to his truck. "Thanks for everything," I say as he opens the door to climb in.

"No problem. Hey, do me a favor, Mags. Make sure you're completely healed before partaking in your next adventure, okay? And please, don't let that adventure be skydiving," he chides.

I playfully roll my eyes since arching my eyebrows is out of the question. "Consider it done," I say, closing his door for him. Pain instantaneously travels from my finger, up my arm, to my brain, which tells me to yowl. Tears well in my eyes. "My finger! Oh, my God! My finger's caught in the door!"

He throws it open, knocking me in the forehead with the window frame in the process. I collapse to the ground. "Fuck! Magnolia. I'm so sorry." He's anxiously assessing the damage. "Don't move."

He pulls a medic bag from his truck, and after tearing a couple of gauze squares from their packages, he plants them in my hand and tells me to hold them tightly against my forehead. That's when I realize I'm bleeding. Good thing I'm already on the ground. I don't even manage a single word before I faint.

SIX

A cool breeze is blowing on my face, and my body feels as though it's gently swaying from side to side. I want to be on my pretend deserted island with Jace, but instead, I'm lying in a small rowboat with my head resting in his lap. His only clothing is a tattered pair of pants, while I'm scantily clad in a homemade bandeau top and skirt made of a few worn strips of fabric. He gently strokes my long, flowing hair as water, the same color of his eyes, softly laps against the small vessel. We're in the middle of nowhere, yet we're not fearful. We're incredibly relaxed, soaking up the cool evening air while delighting in the mere presence of each other.

Smiling down at me, his finger playfully traces down my forehead, over the tip of my nose, and softly across each of my lips. I sigh with content, and taking his hand in mine, I place it on one of my breasts. I feel his leg muscles contract and tighten.

"You like the way they feel, don't you?" I tease.

"Maggie," he breathes. I roll so I can run my hands up the length of his legs. He's so tense and hard as my palm caresses each and every bump leading to the prize at the apex of his thighs.
"Maggie," he calls louder.

"Don't worry, baby. I won't stop until I reach the top," I say with a smirk.

"Maggie, you need to wake up."

My eyes fly open to see Jace jammed up against the driver's side door panel so close that it looks as though he is being smashed by some invisible force. My hands are near his crotch, and it takes me all of half a second to figure out what I'd done. I hide my face in my hands.

"I'm sorry. I'm so sorry. I didn't mean to... I'm so embarrassed."

"Embarrassed about what? Fainting? Don't be. It happens pretty often."

"Fainting? Why are you all scrunched up against the door?" I ask.

"You started to make some pretty strange noises while you were out. I was scared you were going to vomit. The truck, I can clean. Myself? Well, let's just say that I'm not a fan of being puked on."

"So I didn't do anything else?"

Jace looks at me like I'm crazy. "Like what? You've been out cold. I picked up you after you fainted and put you in my truck. We're almost to the urgent care clinic."

"Oh." The memory of everything that had occurred pre-fainting spell suddenly comes back to me, and I realize I'm in pain. Lots of pain! My head and finger are throbbing. I try to see how bad the damage is to my smashed finger, but I discover that Jace has bandaged it.

"It's better that way. You don't want to see it," he says.

"It's that bad?" I ask, suddenly feeling lightheaded again.

"No, it's not bad at all. Swollen and discolored, with a little blood. It's the little bit of blood that I don't want you seeing."

"You're right. It's probably best that it stays covered," I say, pulling it back to my chest.

"Exactly," Jace agrees, taking his eyes from the road long enough to give me a quick wink.

Once we're parked, I try to jump out of the truck, but Jace insists that I sit for a while so I won't crash to the ground once my feet hit the parking lot pavement. He stands in front of me until he's certain that I'm steady on my feet, and he keeps an arm snaked around my waist as we walk into the clinic.

"Big J! Whaddup? You guys implementing casual weekends at the office or something?" a young man wearing navy blue scrubs asks.

"Not quite, Ben. Off duty."

"Oh, my gosh. Just when I thought I couldn't love you more!" a curvy brunette wearing rose colored scrubs squeals. "You're rescuing homeless people during your time off!" She flings her arms around his neck and pelts him with kisses. "Don't worry, ma'am. We're going to get you fixed right on up," she excitedly clucks. She grabs a nearby wheelchair and shoves it behind my knees. I don't even have time to protest before being whisked down a hall and put into a room.

"Dahlia, this is Magnolia. She's not a homeless woman I rescued, she's…"

"Magnolia. How sweet! Isn't it fun being named after a flower? Dahlia. Magnolia. See! I love my flower name. Don't you love yours?" she says in cheery rapid fire. "I'm going to need you to hop on that table right there for me, okay?"

I'm not sure if it's the stress of the day's events, or the fact that she speaks so quickly that my brain needs time to catch up with her words, but it takes me a moment to comprehend what she's asking. Slowly, I stand and shuffle my way towards the exam table.

"Good girl. Right on up there. You're not allergic to anything are you, sweetheart? Jace, do you know if she's allergic to anything?" she asks, arranging some supplies onto a tray. We both shake our heads in response. "Jace, honey, you might want to get some peroxide on those jeans. That blood's gonna stain."

I glance his way, and he's got me in his arms before I hit the floor. I didn't completely go out this time, just some simple knee buckling, but another crash to the ground would have hurt for sure. Without so much as a second thought, he lifts me onto the table.

"Whoops! I didn't realize we had a fainter in our presence," Dahlia says, squirting a stream of liquid from the tip of a syringe. Once she is certain the air bubble is gone, she unzips my skirt, yanks it down a couple of inches, and after a quick swipe of an alcohol pad, she sinks the needle into my hip. "This is a pain reliever. It won't take long to kick in. I'm going to send you for an x-ray of that finger, but first, I want to see your forehead. Okay?"

Even if I wasn't okay with it, there would be no stopping her. She pulls back the gauze, cleans out the wound, and glues it shut. I'm not sure if she takes a breath the entire time she's working on me because she won't stop talking. Jace seems to follow her conversation okay, but I only catch a word or two here and there.

Frustrated that I can't keep up, I decide to completely zone out. *I'm back in the boat with Jace. Oh, yeah. Back in my happy place. This time he's rowing the boat. I lustfully watch as each and every sweaty muscle, from his shoulders to his abdomen, contracts and relaxes as the oar cuts into the water. Feeling brazen, I sexily slow crawl toward him, and his breath catches when I lick my way up his sweaty six-pack. He tosses the oars into the boat, and taking my head in his hands, he pulls me to his lips. His passion devours me, and it's my turn to feel breathless.*

Out of nowhere, a massive wave hits, and the sky turns an ominous shade of gray. The boat is rocking so hard back and forth that we can't keep our balance. I'm tossed overboard, and Jace jumps in to save me. The current tugs us further and further apart, and I lose sight of him. I frantically call for him, and I hear a response, but it doesn't sound like Jace. The voice sounds oddly feminine.

"…and then I told Becky that if she thinks we're ever shopping there again, she's sadly mistaken. Can you believe the nerve of that salesperson? Oh, wait. Look who's waking up! Rise and shine, porcupine! Those pain meds kicked your little hiney didn't they? It's okay. I'm almost finished here. Just a simple little splint for your finger. The break was hairline, so you just wear this splint for a week or so, until the soreness goes away, and you'll be fine. You may or may not lose your fingernail. No worries if you do; it'll grow back."

"Huh?" I ask. Dahlia giggles.

"We'll go over it when I bring you home," Jace says.

"Oh, okay," I say, suddenly flushing because I remember my dream. Jace and Dahlia give no indication that I'd been talking in my sleep, so I begin to relax.

"Thanks for seeing her, Dahlia," he says, tapping the backrest of the wheelchair to signal that I should have a seat.

"It was my pleasure." She bends and places her hands between her knees, so she can be face to face with me. "If you need anything, you be sure to come see me, okay? Be careful out there, Magnolia," she says carefully enunciating each word. Great, first she thinks I'm homeless, and now she thinks I'm stupid. I simply stare at her. "Awww, she's so sweet, Jace. I see why you took a liking to her. We all have that one special patient who stays near and dear to us. Bless her heart. You take care, now." She pats my shoulder. None of that bothers me until she goes on tiptoe and steals a kiss from Jace. Well, I guess it's not technically stealing since he very obviously returns the sign of affection. I look down at my splinted finger, fighting the urge to cry.

Why do I feel this way about a man I barely even know? Maybe it's because he's the only man who has ever acknowledged my existence, to pay attention to me, to talk to me, not at me? Whatever it is, seeing him in the arms of another woman hurts me to my core, but I chastise myself for thinking this way. There is no way in hell a man like Jace would ever in a million years want to be with a screw-up like me. The only way he'll ever be mine is in my dreams, and the sooner I accept that fact, the less it will hurt.

I manage to thank Dahlia before we leave the urgent care clinic, and she gives me a big hug in return. I'm not sure if I like her or hate her at this point. Jace drives me home, and despite my insistence, he remains parked in the driveway, his headlights concentrated on me, as I walk up the steps to my apartment. *One together, two together...* Shit! I miss a step, but catch myself before I take a tumble. He's at my side in no time.

"I'm fine. Really. It was just a missed step. That's why I always keep a death grip on the rail. See? I caught myself. You can leave now. I'm fine." That's what I say out loud. Inside my mind is screaming, *Leave! Leave now!* I can't remember if I picked up my naughty stuff! No one ever visits my apartment, so I leave private things lying about. Not to mention trying to explain my boob wall to someone. Geez! If I see a pair that I like, I cut them out of magazines, or print pictures of them, and pin them to my wall in the hopes that one day I'll be rich and brave enough to afford a pair for myself.

He insists on seeing me inside, and despite my protests, he won't leave. FUCK! I slowly open the door to the apartment, and as is true with human nature, he casually glances around. His eyes instantly settle on my boob wall, and I will the floor to swallow me. Beet red, I look anywhere but at him. In doing so, I notice a porn disc sitting on top of my DVD player, a bullet vibrator and some oil on my nightstand, and the arm of the blowup doll I use to practice kissing skills sticking out from under my bed.

What can one say after such a find? That's why it doesn't upset me in the least when Jace turns on his heel, offers a half-assed wave, and disappears into the darkness. If I ever see him again, it will be too soon.

There's simply no coming back from what has just happened to me.

Just because I don't want to see him in the flesh anymore, doesn't mean I want him gone from my life. The scent of his cologne still hangs in the air, and if I close my eyes, it's almost as if he is with me. I can easily picture the sight of him. I pull off my skirt and turtleneck and slip under the covers. I pull Mr. Loverboy, the blowup doll, from under my bed, gently tucking him in next to me. I rest my head on his shoulder, and eventually, I'm back on the beach with Jace.

When I awaken the next morning, curled in the arms of the blowup doll, the realization hits that I desperately need a man. A *real* man. If I can land a companion, then I won't need to become a serial killer to gain attention.

I'm happy when that thought crosses my mind, since it's pretty damned obvious that I'm not cut out to be a murderer. So, how do I get a man? I have no girlfriends to ask. Dahlia said I could see her if I had any problems, but I don't think that urgency to lose your virginity is what she implied with that statement. Not to mention the fact that Jace has probably told her all about my stash. I need a better plan. Who knows the most about landing a man?

After a few minutes of mulling it over, my eyes light up. A prostitute! They know everything about landing men. I rush over to the freezer and open the box that used to hold fish sticks, but now holds my savings. I'm sure that it's plenty enough to buy some consultation time with a prostitute. I've watched enough TV to know that I'll be charged, even if I only want to talk. I will have to make it worth her time, at least that's what I remember seeing on some show.

Now, where to find a prostitute? That one might take me some time to figure out. In the meantime, I stay confined to my apartment, eating nearly everything in sight from the sheer nervousness of my upcoming encounter. I have no clue what to expect. Julia Roberts was super nice as a prostitute in *Pretty Woman*, the women on the TV show "Cops," not so much. Regardless, I'll have to wait until I don't look like one of the Coneheads before venturing out. Eyebrows and hair might help the man-hunt along just a tad.

seven

Finding a prostitute is easier than one may think. Dressed in my usual attire, but with the addition of a baseball cap and drawn on eyebrows, I visit my favorite porn shop, Fell A She Oh! Candi Jean is behind the counter. She's short, red headed, and has lips so puffed up with collagen that she can barely open her mouth. Donning a naughty school girl costume, she pulls out a tube of pale pink lipstick, uncaps it, and begins to run it across her plump lips. She tosses it into a little bin near the register then turns to see who has entered the store. When she realizes it's just me, she kicks back on her stool and begins to thumb through a magazine.

"Welcome back to Fell A She Oh! Our new arrivals don't come in until tomorrow," she says very monotone and bored. I scan the store, then as an extra precaution, I walk up and down each and every aisle to make sure no one else is in there. Once I'm satisfied, I casually thumb through the trinkets on the counter while Candi Jean continues to ignore me.

I place a pair of naughty dice and a nudie keychain in front of the register, and without looking up from her magazine, Candi Jean passes each over the scanner to ring them up. "Will that be all?" she asks, tossing them into a tiny bag.

"Actually, I was wondering if you could help me with a situation," I say trying to make my voice sound gravelly to disguise it.

"Uh, you know that I already know who you are, right? Why don't you just say what's on your mind without the extra effect?" She tosses down the magazine and looks at me expectantly. "Oh, and whoever did your eyebrows—never go back to that person again. Ever."

"Thanks for the advice," I say, pulling the bill of my cap lower. "What I'm curious about... See, what I need to know is... I'm looking for..."

Candi Jean begins to impatiently tap her foot. "I've rung up the majority of your past purchases. You shouldn't be embarrassed to ask for a thing in this store."

"It's not necessarily in the store. I was sort of hoping you could tell me where I might find a lady of the night," I whisper.

"I wouldn't have guessed that you swung that way, but hey, to each her own. You want to visit Hyde Street if you're looking for high priced model types, Merryland Heights for the mid-priced crack whores, and Laurel Lane for the washed up has-beens desperate for a dollar."

"Thanks," I say, forgetting my purchases behind.

"Uh, hello!" Candi Jean says, holding the bag in the air. I dash back to grab it from her and bolt through the door. Nervous and excited, I take the long route home just so I can swing down Hyde Street. To my dismay, there are no well-dressed women propped against lamp posts, eagerly awaiting the next customer. In fact, the street is essentially barren. I wonder if Candi Jean has fed me a line of bullshit, but then I reach Merryland Heights. Immense, scary looking men hover in the shadows, while scantily clad women of all shapes, sizes, and colors make suggestive gestures towards passersby. There is not a chance in hell that I'll be stopping here for anything! Laurel Lane is the last place on the list, and I'm already apprehensive of what my options will be if it turns out to be a bust.

My thoughts are scattered as I turn down a long street that eventually dead ends. It's not until I'm halfway down the darkened road that I begin to take notice of my surroundings. The people of Laurel Lane must not have very many sunshine yellow Vespas frequent the area, and the once packed street suddenly clears out. The houses are row after row of shotguns, all in various stages of decay. The area reeks of poverty and despair. Babies' cries tangle with dogs' barking, as do the sounds of extra loud televisions blaring through opened windows. Piles of refuse sit in front of nearly every house, making the street smell about as appealing as a sewer treatment plant. Seeing places like this on television and in movies doesn't even come close to the reality of it all.

I spy an abandoned park off to the right, so I carefully guide my scooter between the askew, opened wrought iron gates, and prop it under some trees and bushes in a darkened corner. It's not until I've hung my helmet from the handlebars that I scan the perimeter and realize that this isn't a kiddie park; it's a memorial park! I'm stricken with the overwhelming urge to wet my pants.

Graveyards completely freak me out—like bad. Really, really bad. So bad that I will go miles out of my way to bypass one, and here I am, all alone in the dank darkness, surrounded by row after row of decayed corpses. The fact that there is a thick layer of concrete, marble, or granite between me and said corpses does absolutely nothing to calm my nerves. My knees start to jiggle, my mouth runs dry, and when a leaf blows up against my leg, I bolt as though my life depends on it.

In my haste to retreat, my skirt snags on one of the frayed iron bars, and I take a tumble on the sidewalk. I survey the scuffs on my knees and right elbow. They're mild abrasions, but they burn like hell! Trying to shake off the trauma I just experienced, I skirt the edge of the shadows as I continue further down the street.

After three blocks, I notice a woman standing at

one of the corners. She's leaned over, talking into the window of a pickup truck that is more rust than metal. Thick gray clouds of exhaust puff from the tailpipe, obscuring my view, but I hear her loudly telling the driver that he can't afford her.

Doing my best to disappear into the night, I push my back against the frame of one of the nearby houses and slowly inch my way closer to the action. The truck takes off, and the extra tall woman is left coughing and hacking courtesy of the truck's pollution heavy wake. I'm almost parallel to her, yet she has no clue I'm here. I feel empowered, like a lioness gearing up for a hunt. Why? I have no clue, but I sure am enjoying the new sensation.

As soon as the coughing spell eases up, she hocks a loogie onto the ground, pulls her oversized bag tightly onto her shoulder, and then sashays down the street. Tailing her, I sprint from shadow to shadow, carefully observing her every move. She's not nearly as tall as I had originally assumed; the majority of her height comes from the giant, platinum blonde beehive hairdo she's sporting. Her wardrobe consists of an extremely short red leather cut-out dress, black patent leather stiletto heels, and black thigh highs that have more holes than fabric. The bag she clutches close to her body doesn't match her ensemble in any way, shape, or form, and is a floral needlepointed monstrosity unlike anything I've ever seen.

She continues further and further down the street, moving into an area where the streetlights no longer offer soft illumination of the area. I still hear the *click, click, click, click* of her heels against the pavement; it serves as a beacon, drawing me closer and closer. A car, headlights off, slowly rolls up alongside her, but as soon as she leans into the passenger side window, the car zooms off, tires squealing against the pavement.

"Well, fuck you, too!" she yells towards the rapidly disappearing taillights. The driver makes a rapid U-turn in the middle of the street and barrels back in our direction. A young man clinging to the top of the car sits in the frame of the passenger side window, and once the car rolls to a stop, he yells, "Cougar? You passed that shit up about twenty years ago, grandma! Do the world a favor and retire that snatch!" He bangs his palm against the roof of the car, while peals of laughter echo through the night.

"What's wrong? Afraid you might try it and like it? Just as well; you can't afford me. Your entire Taco Hell paycheck wouldn't even cover a hand job from me."

"Bitch! I don't work at no taco place. I'm an entrepreneur."

"That means you have no paycheck. You're wasting my time. Fuck off."

The carload of boisterous men taunts her further. She threatens them with bodily harm, which they laugh at until she starts digging around in her oversized bag and pulls out a butterfly knife that she expertly manipulates to ready the blade.

"Dude, she's like fucking Bruce Lee or some shit. Ride!"

"Go! Go! Go!" the guy hanging out the passenger window yells, banging his palm against the roof, this time to express urgency. The tires squeal as the car races down the darkened, deserted street. All becomes quiet again, except for the sound of the occasional dog barking or cat meowing. The woman mumbles under her breath and still has no clue that I'm near her in the shadows. I realize she's crying, and my nurturing side wants to comfort her. Stepping out of the shadows, I inch toward her. I reach for her, resting my hand upon her shoulder, when I hear a *zap*, feel a supercharged jolt of electricity, and then go for a swim in a sea of darkness.

*****

The first of the five senses that comes back to me is smell. There's an odd odor around: a mix of cigarette smoke, patchouli, and bacon, with slight undertones of mentholated muscle liniment. Next is my hearing. I'm pretty sure a western is playing on a TV in the background, or at least I hope that's where the sound of clomping horse hooves and the *pow-pow* of pistol fire is coming from. I slowly open my eyes, and as things come into focus, I see a tile ceiling that has seen far better days. I'm sure it was once white, but between the smoke which hangs heavily in the air, and the obvious water damage, it's now a dingy yellow-brown. Without moving my head, I dart my eyes around the room, desperately trying to figure out where in the hell I'm at.

The room is relatively dark, except for the little bit of light spilling from the television. I'm lying on a lumpy rust-orange velour sofa, and to my right is an avocado green and chocolate brown striped recliner rapidly rocking back and forth. I can't see who is seated in it because the chair's back is facing me. I know it's occupied, not just from the rocking, but from the puff of smoke that rises upwards every thirty seconds or so.

I sit up, and even though I do it slowly, I feel a sudden rush to my head. Grasping my forehead, I wait until the sensation passes before moving again. The chair spins around, and with a lit cigarette one hand and a stun gun in the other, the platinum blonde granny gives me the stink eye.

"Ha-how did I get here?" I softly ask, gently raising my hands in the air.

"How the fuck do you think you got here?" she asks in a gravelly voice.

I nervously shake my head. "I don't know."

"I dragged your ass. My turn to ask a question. Why were you sneaking around in the dark in this hood? I ain't never seen you around here before."

"I-I was…" The words won't come out. All I can concentrate on is the stun gun she keeps fiddling with.

"This scare you?" she asks, removing her hand

from the stun gun to snuff her cigarette out against the sole of her stiletto heel. She tosses the butt into an old coffee can near her chair.

"Yes. I can't say that I remember very much about what happened."

"Give it about ten minutes. It'll start coming back to you. Your brain waves are all jumbled up. It's normal. What's your name?"

"Magnolia Berrybush."

"Shit. That jolt must've scrambled you up real bad for you to be spitting out nonsense like that."

"No, that's my name. I'm sure of it," I say, looking toward the floor.

"Berrybush. I've heard that name before. Where?" She looks in deep thought for about twenty seconds. "I'll get you your money faster than green grass through a goose! His name is Berrybush. Murray! Yeah, Murray Berrybush, the fat attorney who dresses like Colonel Sanders. I love his commercials. Awww, fuck me," she groans. "I just stunned the relative of one of them dirty trial lawyers. I'm so screwed. I ain't got a pot to piss in, lady. Have mercy, please. See? Look around. Nothing. But if you see something you like, maybe we can work out a deal?"

"I don't want your things."

She sucks on her teeth. "Oh, so it's gonna be like that? Planning on making a fool outta me in court? Fine. Do what you gotta do, but I can promise you this…"

I hold up my hand to stop her. "Wait. I'm not taking you to court. I'm not suing, and I'm not telling my father about this, so relax."

"Your father? Oh great. No, oh wait! What's the daughter of the most well-known attorney in South Louisiana doing in my neighborhood? You have to be up to no good, especially with the get up you got going. I'm sorry, honey, but you need to fire your beautician."

I reach up and notice that the bandana/ball cap combo is gone from my head. Instead, I feel a stretch of stubble on the top and the ring of dishevelment around the sides.

"I did it to myself," I say softly.

"Why?"

"It was an accident."

"Why don't you just shave the rest to match the top, that way it'll all grow back at one time?"

I'm embarrassed to tell her that I hadn't thought of that, so I sort of shrug my shoulders in response. She rises from her chair and takes a seat on the cushion beside me. I'm able to see that she's not nearly as old as I first thought. In fact, it's her hairstyle and makeup that make her appear aged beyond her years.

"So, how much you gonna give me to keep my mouth shut?" she asks with a smirk.

"What?" Nerves start to get the best of me, and I start to giggle.

"Hush money. I'm sure your father wouldn't

appreciate it getting out that his daughter frequents this neighborhood. Might hurt his career," she says with a devious grin.

The nervous giggles turn to full on tears. "No, please, no. My parents don't have much to do with me as it is. If I get caught doing something that will put him in an unfavorable light, he'll have no problem alienating me. I have nothing. No friends, no boyfriend, no job… I lost that a couple of weeks ago and still haven't had the guts to tell my parents. They will toss me on the street without batting an eye, and they'll call it a life lesson to boot. Please, please, please, don't do this to me." I lower my head to my lap and sob uncontrollably.

"Stop that!" she fusses. "Stop it now. You sound like a dying goose. Shut up. The neighbors are gonna call the cops."

"Police! *Eeeuhhh!*" I wail. "Not the police!" I release a loud snort and sniff before I start sobbing again.

"Shut it! Now!" she says, tugging on the collar of my turtleneck to pull me so she can look me in the face. "Shhhh!"

Swallowing hard, I nod my head and wipe the tears from my face. "You're not going to tell?"

"You sure are a pathetic one, aren't you?" The woman kicks off her stilettos and tucks her feet underneath her. "Spill. Tell it to me. Give me all of your ugly."

"I don't know what you're talking about."

"Bullshit. You might be goofy as hell, but you're not dumb. You came down here looking for one of two things: a prostitute or drugs. Clearly, drugs are not your thing, so it has to be a prostitute. Why would a woman, I'm guessing early to mid-thirties..." She pauses, and I nod. "...be on the prowl for a prostitute? You need some advice that only a whore can give? Judging from the circa 1970s bush fro you're sporting under that skirt, I think it's safe to say that you've never been with a man. Am I right?"

My eyes widen with horror, and I turn a lovely shade of vermilion. "I-I don't know a lot about... Why were you looking up my skirt?"

"It kinda rode up when I was dragging you in here. It's not like I went in search of it. It just kinda popped out and said hi. Another thing you might not know is that a lot of women shave their legs."

"Yeah, I know, but I figure there's no point. The only person to get close enough to see it has been you."

She turns sideways on the sofa so she can prop her elbow on the back of it. "Have you ever had a boyfriend?"

"One."

"Tell me about him."

"I don't think I want to."

"Why not? It's not often that I get the hankering to help someone, but you are very obviously a lost soul in need of some Honey Bear intervention."

"Honey Bear?"

"That's me. Honey LeReaux. You know, like, *row, row, row your boat gently up my…* Oh, never mind. The guys love it, but it's obviously lost on you."

"Well, Ms. Honey…"

"Don't you go calling me Ms. anything. Honey's the name."

"Okay, Honey."

Honey smiles and nods her approval.

"The relationship with the only boyfriend I've ever had lasted a total of twenty minutes," I admit.

"Did you fuck him?"

Though still a little shocked by Honey's potty mouth, I feel less intimidated by her constant barrage of questions. "No, but he tried to kiss me."

"Would that have been your first kiss?"

"Yes."

"How long ago did all of this happen?"

"A few weeks ago."

She looks at me with intrigue. "You're understated, but not ugly. What's wrong with you?"

"I wish I knew," I say a little depressed.

"Naw, naw, naw, now none of that. No feeling sad over the past. If I dwelled on my past, I'd have killed myself long ago. Let's agree that we're going to focus on the present and future only. Deal?"

"Deal?" I say with a slightest of smiles. "Thank you for this, Honey."

"For what? I ain't done nothin'."

"You're treating me like a person. You're

interacting with me, actually listening to me."

"Here I woulda thunk that you, growing up with rich parents and such, you would've had it all. I guess the old sayin' is right, money can't buy happiness. You're about the saddest soul I've come across in ages. I need to hear how this happened."

Standing, I turn my back to her so she won't see the tears starting to well in the corners of my eyes. "This isn't a good idea. I came here with the intention of receiving information on how to land a man, not to get therapy."

Honey stands behind me and gently pushes some of the longer strands of hair from my shoulder. "If you want a man, you should start with fixing yourself. To do that, you need to let someone in. It's not something you can do alone; otherwise you wouldn't be here. Look, I can understand your not wanting life advice from a washed up whore, but when it comes to living life, I've done, seen, and experienced it all. I might be able to help."

"Why would you want to help me? What's in it for you?"

"Nothing really. I don't know why, but I like ya. You're kinda like a pathetic stray desperate for some lovin'."

"I thought you wanted me to feel better about myself."

"First lesson: people are mean. Don't take anything people say personally. Chances are, there is an issue of some sort within them, but they're taking it out on you. Misery sure does love company."

"Is that why those guys were so mean to you earlier?" I ask.

"Exactly. The loud mouth feels the need to stand out in the crowd. Probably one of the youngest in a sea of siblings who never got much attention unless he acted out. A jackass who is trying to be a leader because he's sick of being a follower. The others, well, they're just along for the ride because they're bored."

"You could tell all of that from that one ride by?"

After lighting a cigarette, she eases back onto the sofa. "Maybe. Or maybe I know his momma. It doesn't matter. Point is, I know shit; you need to know shit. You want help or not?"

"I do."

"Good." She blows out a thick cloud of smoke and starts rummaging through stack after stack of junk. "We're gonna straighten out that hair situation of yours first thing, just as soon as I find my damned scissors. You can fill me in on your story while I'm fixing that mess. You can't go through life with a reverse Mohawk. I won't let you. Trust me. This is for the best," she says, holding up a massive pair of sewing shears.

Gulp!

Honey slices through the last of the hair and holds a handheld mirror inches from my face. As I run my fingers through the bristly stubble, I feel like *Les Miserables'* Fantine, post hair donation. I'm not impressed with my reflection, and it shows on my face.

"You watch and see how fast that's gonna grow back," Honey assures me. "I should know, been there myself. There was a lice situation back in the eighties; well, I completely de-haired myself, and it was the best thing I ever coulda done. My hair grew in a lot thicker and two shades darker. I turned a lot of heads back in those days."

I scrunch my drawn on eyebrows as I try to picture a young, bald Honey LeReaux. "De-haired? That's a term I've never heard used for a shaved head."

"I don't know all them fancy words, and I ain't talking about just my head. What do you call it? I was exfoliated?"

"Epilated?"

"Yeah, maybe that's it. You gotta understand; that was before you could get a wax from every corner in town. I had to recruit some close friends to give me a hand. That's neither here nor there, I suppose. Ancient history now." She tosses the shears into a kitchen drawer then lights up a fresh cigarette.

"All of your hair was gone?"

"From head to toe," she said, taking a drag.

"Okay, what's a wax and what does it have to do with epilation?" My inquiry earns me a dropped jaw from Honey. She stops rolling the cigarette lighter between her fingers and flings it to the far end of the table before taking my chin in her hand. She studies my face through partially squinted lids.

"Of course you wouldn't know what a wax is. That's a pretty thick mustache you're sporting there, not to mention that pile of carpet you've got hanging to your knees down there."

I pull my face away quickly to cover my upper lip with my fingers. "I'd appreciate it if you'd quit talking about my privates. Besides, how's wax supposed to help with that?"

She slowly shakes her head from side to side. "I can't believe I'm actually explaining this to a grown woman. Wow, okay. What you do is you go to a place that offers waxing services, or in my case, you get a friend who ain't ashamed to get up in there. The wax goes into a warmer to melt, a layer is spread, and then covered with a strip of fabric. Those pesky hairs are ripped right on out."

"Ripped out! By the root? And women actually pay for that torture?" I ask, unable to fully comprehend the concept.

"All the time," Honey answers matter of factly.

"What happened to razors? That's what I used the last time; I just shaved."

"Oh, for legs and pits, yeah, lots still use razors for that, but I'd hope you wouldn't take a razor to your eyebrows. Kinda hard to get a good arch with a razor, much less the chance you take of slicing off your eyelid. You really don't know any of this?"

"I notice that other women look different from me, but I never really gave much thought as to how they got that way."

Honey looks deep in thought as the cigarette between her lips quickly decimates to a long, hollow cylinder of ash. "I don't know why, but I feel like I should help you. Maybe it's because I've always had a soft spot for lost causes."

"Hey! I have feelings, you know?"

She's unfazed by my outburst. "Lesson two: you need to thicken up that thin skin. You can't run and hide from the world; you need to own it. To make it your bitch."

"I tried to make my mark on the world. I walked on the wild side, and all it got me was hurt."

"Really? The wild side, eh? I find that hard to believe. Tell me what you consider wild."

"I can't," I shyly reply.

She sucks on her teeth. "That's what I thought."

Feeling the need to defend myself, I carelessly blurt, "Oh, yeah? Well, I almost killed a man. Is that wild enough for you?"

She chuckles. "Who hasn't? Most of 'em are scum bags."

"No, I'm serious. I almost killed a guy by stabbing him in the neck."

All signs of being amused flee from her face, and she nervously scans the room. "What do you mean you stabbed a guy in the neck?"

"Nothing," I quickly answer.

"Oh, no! You can't drop a bomb like that and think that I'm just gonna let you strut on outta here."

"It was more of an accident than an actual stabbing, okay? He was really old, and I had a hobby knife in my hand. He spun around, and I got him in the neck."

"And why were you holding a hobby knife next to an old guy's throat?"

"I can't tell you."

"Why not?" Honey asks, sitting back in the seat and crossing her arms over her chest. "If I had any desire to snitch on you, don't you think I'd have done it already? You just as well quit playing these games and fess up. I'm giving you fair warning, there are ways of getting people to talk. We can do this the easy way, or we can do this the hard way. It's up to you."

"I don't want to say because you're going to laugh at me," I confess, resting my head on the table.

Honey lights a fresh cigarette, and once she exhales a cloud of bluish-gray smoke, she stares me down. "I won't laugh."

"I think you will."

"I think you better tell me something worth hearing before I cram my fist down that scrawny throat of yours." She leans forward, producing a rolled up fist that she shakes near my face.

"I thought people might finally notice me if I became a serial killer." Words shoot out of my mouth in rapid fire staccato.

"You? A serial killer? No way, no how, no, no, no. That's the stupidest thing I've ever heard," she says with a hearty chuckle.

"You're laughing. You said you wouldn't."

"Life lesson number three: people lie. They do it all of the time, so expect it, be ready for it, and be prepared to do it yourself."

"Lying is so... so... dishonest."

"You lead an incredibly sheltered life, don't you?"

"I guess I've never really given it much thought."

"Well, I'm not gonna bullshit you. If you want to get noticed, killing people ain't the way to go about it. Sure, you'll get attention, but that ain't the kinda attention you're looking for. You wouldn't last one night in a women's prison. Now tell me, whose attention are you trying to get? Your parents'? A man's? Whose?"

"Everyone's, I suppose."

She remains silent for a brief moment. "Yeah, okay. Let's start with something a little less ambitious. Stand up."

Completely unsure of what's about to happen, I slowly do as she requests.

Still holding her cigarette between her lips, while it wildly bobs up and down as she speaks, she says, "Hold your arms out to the side." She rises from her seat, and starting with the top of my head, she begins her assessment. "Hair. You'll have to wear a wig for a while, but that's okay. I've got plenty to choose from. Hmmmm. You might do well as a red head, or maybe a blonde? Gotta get you away from that boring color. Make up is a must. Your bone structure is fabulous, so fabulous that I'm willing to bet that it was bought."

"I had an accident not too long ago."

"That makes sense."

"What do you mean?"

"Well, you're plain Jane, but you're not repulsive. It doesn't make sense to me. Even with no head hair, too much hair everywhere else, no eyebrows, no makeup, and no experience, there should still be men trying to get up that skirt of yours. You gotta pic of what you looked like before the accident? Just so I can see what you started with."

"I never know if I should be insulted by your comments or not," I say with a touch of ire.

"I just say what's on my mind. Take it as you want it."

I give a little sigh as I retrieve my phone and scroll through my pictures. They are primarily artistic shots of inanimate objects that I find interesting, but towards the end of the list, I find a rare selfie from when I unsuccessfully tried the "duck face" that was popular at the time. I turn the screen to Honey, and she rips the phone from my hands.

"*This*. Is. You? How did you manage to eat with those chompers? Obviously, you didn't judging by the size of you in this picture. Your bones are sticking out everywhere. And that bun. Please don't tell me you wore that in public. It's bigger than your entire head! Eyebrows; you realize that they shouldn't look like one giant caterpillar in the middle of your forehead, don't you? Wow. There's so much wrong with this picture that I don't even know what to talk about next."

I snatch the phone back from her. "Hey, feelings! Remember?"

"Hey, you need to toughen up. Remember?"

I plop down in the chair and dejectedly place my head on my forearm. I feel Honey softly rubbing my back.

"What you need to realize is that the person in that picture is gone. Not many people get the opportunity you've been handed. You get to start again with a clean slate. New face, new teeth, no baggage from the past. You can't afford to waste no more time. You've been a woman for a long time, Magnolia, but you been livin' the life of a girl. It's time to grow up, and I'm gonna help you. First, I'm gonna help with the outside, and then we're gonna keep with baby steps. We're gonna get you your first kiss."

I lift my head. "I suppose you're going to peddle me out to the first person who's willing to do it?"

"No, you're gonna pay for it. Your first kiss should be nice, special, experimental, and awkward— when you're a kid. You're in your thirties, and you well but bypassed that window long ago. Now you need a man who will kiss and NOT tell. It'll likely be a disaster, but you gotta get it outta the way."

"What are you going to make me do?"

"We're gonna head to Avery Street where some of the man whores hang out. You're gonna find one you like, slip 'em ten bucks, and he's gonna shove his tongue so far down your throat that you'll wonder if your tonsils are still there. You'll get weak-kneed, but try to pay attention to what he's doing. Mimic what he does. Notice what feels good and what feels icky."

"That sounds like a whole lot to remember. If that much work goes into kissing, how much work goes into sex?"

"Magnolia, that's not something we can discuss quickly. You're talking about sessions that have to be broken up and discussed individually. We'll have to cover undressing, foreplay, toys, oral… The list goes on and on, and that's before we even THINK about penetration."

"The porn films make it look so easy. If you're bendy, sex rocks."

"So you're basing all sex on porn? You realize those things are staged, right? Real life don't work that way. Every guy don't have a twelve inch penis, not every bit of sex feels so good that you can hardly contain yourself, most people don't have multiple orgasms, and even though it's been a long time for me, fucking and making love are pretty different. You don't see that so much in the porn films. I might be a jaded old prostitute with a huge chip on her shoulder, but I still hope that somebody will come along, sweep me off of my feet, and save me from this shitty ass life I've created for myself."

"I guess I've been so preoccupied with figuring out how to lose my virginity that I never thought of what would happen after that. Truly, I never envisioned a man being interested in me at all. I kinda thought that if it ever happened, it would be because some random drunk guy lost a bet and had to sleep with me as punishment. It would be a quick, one-time thing. At least that's how I envisioned it. You know the reaction you had when you saw my picture from before? Well, that's pretty much what I've had happen to me all my life."

Honey's eyebrows scrunched together. "Let me tell ya something. There ain't no one to blame but yourself. I could be feeling sorry for you with that sad sob story you givin' me, but all it does is get me mad. It don't matter how beaver-toothed, boney, and plain Jane you are; that ain't no excuse to sit back and let life pass you by! Inner beauty is way more special than what a person wears on the outside. Sure, we enhance our outer beauty, but it's just that—an enhancement. The real deal is on the inside. You were scared to share your light with the world, so you told yourself that you was happy being a nobody, but the problem with being a nobody is you get lonely. You're a chicken shit, and because of that you let life pass you by. You've been given a second chance that a lotta people don't get; you better make the most of it. You gotta expect better, want better, demand better, but in return, you gotta give of yourself, too. You gotta make your mark on the world by letting your inner light shine, Magnolia. You can't hide in the shadows no more."

Tears start to roll down my cheeks. "I've been to therapists, counselors, and doctors; none of them got it right, but you did. I'm scared. I'm scared of everything, so I do my best to become invisible. I wanted more, but not badly enough to go out and get it. But not too long ago, something happened to change that, and now I want it all."

"What was the spark that set off this new way of thinkin?"

I shake my head. "I can't believe I'm telling you all of this. I've known you for what? An hour?"

"What's that got to do with anything? How many hours you spend with them fancy doctors and ain't got an ounce of help? Let's finish this. What got your motor runnin'? I got my speculations, but I want to hear it from you first."

"A touch," I answer softly while recalling the memory.

Honey snaps her fingers to draw me back to reality. "You need to give me more than that. A touch? What kind of a touch? Who did the touchin'?"

"The reason my face and nose were redone is because I had an accident. I was picked up by an ambulance crew, and when one of the medics touched me, I felt something new. Something that made me take notice, even in the midst of dealing with excruciating pain."

"How'd he act around you?"

"He was nice, *and* he talked to me! That's something most don't bother to do."

"How you know he ain't interested? Maybe that was his way of feeling you out?"

"No. No way. This guy is like model gorgeous, and besides, he's got a beautiful girlfriend, a physician's assistant named Dahlia. He brought me to the urgent care clinic where she works, and they practically made out in the exam room once she finished fixing me up."

"Is that the time you hurt your face?"

"No, this was a different time."

"Hmmmm. Well, I'm not going back on the street tonight. You just as well crash here if you'd like. It ain't much, but it's mostly clean. The bedroom's usually for clients. I sleep on the sofa, but I suppose I can make an exception for tonight and let you have the couch."

"Thanks for the offer, but I don't want to put you out."

"You want to go wandering around out there at this time of night?"

"Not really," I answer truthfully.

"Smart. It's no trouble. Plus, if you stay, we can start your makeover tomorrow. I wonder what we can use to get those shitty drawn-on eyebrows off of your face? We'll try rubbing alcohol first, and if that don't work, baby oil. Now where'd I put the baby oil?" she asks, picking up bottle after bottle of massage oil, lube, and novelty products to scan the labels. I'm instantly intimidated by her vast collection.

"Honey, I've answered a lot of questions about me, what about you? How long have you been a hooker?"

"Too long, sugar. Too fuckin long," she says, still scanning the bottles. She finally finds what she was looking for, smiling as she turns to show it to me. "Got it." She can tell from the look on my face that I want to know more. She pulls another cigarette from the pouch and places it between her lips. "Since I was seventeen," she says, smoke billowing from her mouth.

"Seventeen? So young?"

"Well, when all your family except for your ninety year old great-grandma splits, you don't really get left with a lotta options once she kicks the bucket. Seventeen—too old for foster care, too young to support yourself any legal way. I got her house, but with that I also got property taxes, utility bills, maintenance costs, and a buttload of other responsibilities teenagers don't give a shit about. I sold the house and had a pretty chunk of change in my bank account. Vultures came out of the woodwork, all eager to help me spend the money, but none willing to stick around once it was gone. By the end of that year, I was broke, had no place to live, and no friends to go to for help. My last couppla dollars was spent rentin' a room at a rundown motel on the outskirts of town. One night, I went to get a coke from the machine, and while I'm out there, this man offers me money for sex. It was enough to pay for another week's rent, plus I had a little extra for food. I kept doin' it after that, never givin' it a second thought. It is what it is—a job. How I make a living. How I survive."

"Did you ever think about giving it up?" I ask.

She stares off in the distance, takes a slow pull from her cigarette, and then glances back my way.

"Every single day; just not in the cards."

I slowly allow the sadness of her life story to fully absorb. "I'm sorry."

"Nothin' for you to be sorry about. I told ya because ya asked, not because I wanted your sympathy. I done alright for myself. It might not look that way so much right now, but back in the eighties and nineties, I was one of them high-priced Hyde street girls." She walks over to a shelf in the far corner of the room and brings back a framed picture. In it is a beautiful woman who can easily grace the cover of any magazine. Her golden blonde hair is twisted into a sophisticated updo, her lips are stained ruby red to match her satiny cocktail dress, and her hazel eyes sparkle with the slightest hint of mischief. She is an alluring woman whom I'd give anything to look like. Sporting a huge, drunken grin, a man sloppily wearing his tuxedo has her pulled close to him as he raises a bottle of some sort of clear alcohol to the photographer. I study the picture a little longer and realize that I recognize the man from the big screen.

"Is that…"

"Yep," Honey says with a smile. "His reputation is well deserved."

"Who is that with him?" I ask.

"And, that's the downside of this line of work. It robs you of your youth, your soul, your desire to strive for better. Once you been to the top, there's no way in hell you're gonna get back up there again. Too many younger ones with tight asses and perky tits willing to claw their way into the top spot, and let's just say that the tumble down is far from pleasant and really hard to adjust to. That woman in the picture, it's me," Honey says with a sigh.

The longer I look, the more I'm able to recognize certain features. It sure as hell was Honey, but the years have been far from kind to her. Unsure of what to say, I slowly hand the picture back to her.

"Hey, enough with the look. I still got that dress in my closet. Wanna try it on? You got a pretty rockin' bod going there. How'd you get that, by the way? You looked like a stick figure in that before pic you showed me."

I shrug my shoulders. "Stress eating, I think. Oh, and when my jaw was wired shut, all I could have was liquids for a couple of weeks. I might have gone a little crazy with the pizza and fast food once I was able to eat solid foods again."

"Well, looks like it did ya some good. You filled out in all the right places near as I can tell. Go ahead, take your clothes off and let me see what you have to work with."

My throat feels like it's closing up. "What? I don't think…"

Honey gives me a confused look. "You've never changed clothes in front of another woman before? Come on? Gym class? Locker room? Dressing room?"

I frantically shake my head from side to side.

"Big Daddy petitioned for me to be exempt from gym class, and all my clothes are mail order."

"Seriously?" Honey asks. I nod. "Have you ever been naked around anyone else?"

"Not since I was a baby. I almost got naked for Sunny's art class, but stuff kinda happened before I got my robe off."

"Who's Sunny?"

"My mother. She teaches art lessons in the nude."

"But you shy away from nudity? Seems like you'd be more open to it."

"Sunny's body is bought and paid for. She's got a lot to show off."

"What's so bad about your body? You look pretty good to me, and I should know."

"Really? You don't think that men will find this repulsive?" I ask, flicking my hand through the air along the length of my body.

"Take off the turtleneck. A little helpful hint—no one wears that shit anymore. Don't ever wear one again. And that skirt… We need to do some wardrobe updating ASAP."

I slowly pull the turtleneck over my head, and before I get it halfway up, I hear, "Whoa! Okay, I just got a glimpse of your pits. Sugar, I mean this in the nicest way possible, but I want you to march your ass into that bathroom, find the pack of razors that are in the second drawer to the left, and use every last one of 'em if you hafta getting rid of that forest under your

arms and up and down your legs. Go on. Go.
There's a robe on the back of the door that you can
put on once you're less bushy."

I should probably be offended, but I'm not.
Finally, for the first time in my life, someone is taking
the time to show me girly things, and I'm beginning to
get excited it. Obviously, Honey sees something in
me that others don't. To her, I'm not a lost cause. I
can't help but grin as I shut the door to the tiny
bathroom.

nine

The problem with not shaving on a regular basis is that lack of experience is painful. My underarms are smooth, my legs bare, and my lady part nicely trimmed thanks to a pair of scissors found in the drawer with the razors. Unfortunately, there is a nick or cut every inch or so in each place the razor touched, and the cuts won't stop bleeding. I feel woozy quite a few times, but thankfully, I don't pass out. Grabbing a roll of toilet tissue, I begin to wrap myself like a mummy. Around and around each leg I roll, and the tissue starts to look like a candy cane. With two giant wads under each armpit, I'm pretty sure I've done all I can to contain the bloodshed.

I can't sit or the tissue around my legs will come loose. My only option is to stand in sort of a sumo wrestler-ish semi-squat while I wait for the bleeding to stop.

"Sugar, you sure have been in there…" Without so much as a knock, Honey pops her head in the door. I turn to her, doe in the headlights look plastered upon my face. "I don't hardly ever get left speechless. You nearly did it. What the fuck are you doing? Are you trying to take a shit on my floor? And what's with the toilet paper leggings? Did you seriously cut yourself that bad?"

I pluck the two wads from under my armpits and toss them into the trash. After, I nervously yank the tissue from the top of my thigh and begin to unravel it as quickly as possible from around my leg. "Yes, I cut myself that badly. May I please have some privacy?" I snap.

"You really wear these?" she asks holding out the bra and panty set that I had placed on the edge of the sink. I reach out to snatch them from her, but she dangles them just out of my reach. "My grandma didn't even wear bras this boring, and this…this gives new meaning to granny panties. There's a small country out there missin' its flag."

I angrily fist my hands on my hips. "Are you done?"

"No," she says snidely. "I was gonna tell you that you got nice tits. They shouldn't be imprisoned in that white straightjacket ya call a bra. Let's see if we can put 'em in something that shows them off. Oh, and nice job on the trim down below. I'm still introducing you to the waxer, though."

"You really think my boobs are okay?" I ask, turning so I could see them in the mirror.

"Sure. What do you think is wrong with them?"

"I have a wall of boobs at my apartment. I know it sounds strange, but I find boobs I like and I cut them out of magazines or print pictures of them so I can pick my favorite when I get brave enough to have the surgery to get them."

"I've heard of people doing that, but they usually don't hang 'em on their wall as far as I know. Usually, they just keep 'em in a binder or something."

If ever there were a time that warranted a face palm, this is it. *A binder? Why in the hell did I NOT consider that?* I struggle for a response, but it's unnecessary because Honey is already in her bedroom fumbling through the drawers of her dresser. She tosses me a black lace bra and panty set that still has the tags attached. "Try those on. I just got 'em yesterday."

While I'm dressing, she opens her closet and exposes a plethora of mannequin heads topped with wigs of various hair styles and colors. "Let's try ya as a red head," she says, pulling a copper colored wig cut in a short bob from the mannequin farthest to the right. I slide it over my shorn scalp, adjust it a bit, and look in Honey's direction. "Nope. It don't look right. Take it off, and we'll try blonde."

She holds out a super long, curly number for me to wear. Once it's in place, I turn to her for feedback. "The color is better, but the curls are too much.

Humor me and put this one on." She gives me a jet black wig, and once it's in place, the silky, straight hair falls just below my shoulder blades. "Oh, dear God," Honey says with an almost foreboding tone.

"It's that bad?" I say reaching up to snatch the hair from my head.

"Stop!" Honey shouts. "Don't move! Don't even breathe."

"What's wrong?" I fearfully ask as my mind races through the possibilities. Honey dashes off into the bathroom and returns with a makeup bag. I feel her penciling in the area where my eyebrows once were, and after sliding a layer of lipstick across my lips, she tells me to rub them together.

"Mother fucker," Honey mumbles under her breath.

"It's hopeless. Just let me go back to my apartment where I can disappear…" Honey firmly grips my shoulders and spins me around to face the mirror. I barely recognize the reflection staring back at me. The dark hair makes my emerald green eyes pop with color, and the brows that Honey drew frame their wide, almond shape. Red makes my lips look plumper and fuller, creating a pouty effect. Convinced that Honey had somehow played a fast one on me, I slowly reach out to touch the glass.

"You're a hottie. Who knew that *this* was under all that body hair and fonky clothes! Just call me the miracle worker," Honey says with a chuckle. I do a slow spin, taking in every inch of the transformation.

I actually look like some of the women I'd seen in the porn movies and magazines, and not the nasty ones, the pretty ones! I continue to stare at my reflection when Honey reaches up to remove the wig.

"What did you do that for?" I ask. The spell was broken. I was no longer an exotic beauty. Fantine is back, but in lacy lingerie.

"Cause no matter how beautiful and sexy you get, the fact remains that you're inexperienced and in no way ready for the attention you'll get. I gotta get you ready before lettin' you loose in the world."

"How do you do that?" I inquire.

"We stick to the plan. I'm gonna let you borrow some not so frumpy clothes, and we're gonna take a ride to the west side of Merryland Heights."

"I thought that Merryland Heights is where the crack whores hang out," I say, repeating what Candi Jean from the adult shop had told me.

"That's over on the east side, and how'd ya know about that?" Honey asks.

I give her a shrug. "I heard someone talking about it one day."

"Hmmm. Well, my friend Dan Wan will probably be our best hope. Let's go pay him a visit. I'll drive," she says tossing me a pair of blue jeans and a plain brown t-shirt. The jeans are too big, the shirt a little more snug than I normally wear, but Honey gives me no time to search for something that might fit better.

She locks the door of the dilapidated shotgun

house and uses a shiny, silver key to unlock the passenger door of the mammoth 1974 Chrysler New Yorker parked in the drive. At one time, its color was likely gold, but from what I can see courtesy of the dim streetlight, the exterior seems to be primarily body filler and rust. Once we're both seated on the tattered bench seat, Honey turns the key. After a brief hesitation, the car roars to life; thick heavy plumes of smoke barrel from the exhaust and pollute the clammy night air. Teeth jarring vibrations become worse when she puts the car into gear, but Honey doesn't seem to mind. She mashes on the gas pedal, and after a slight hiccup, the car screeches from the driveway and noisily fumigates the neighborhood as we leave it behind.

There is no way I'm going to attempt to talk over the noise of the engine and randomly back-firing exhaust, so I'm silent all the way to Merryland Heights. Honey parks the tank near the curb and under a tree that grows in a vacant lot. My brain is still vibrating when she tells me to follow her.

She crosses the street and hangs a right into the first alleyway she approaches. Everything looks deserted upon our arrival, but the further we drift down the smelly, litter-filled alley that is actually just the rear of a line of restaurants and bars, more and more people become visible.

"Hey, who y'all lookin' for?" a tall black man wearing red fishnets and a black leather bikini asks.

"Dan Wan," Honey says never giving the guy a

second look.

"He's over there," Mr. Leather Bikini says with a playful point in the right direction.

"Thanks, sugar," Honey says with a wink.

"Anytime, honeybunch. Toodles."

I'm still trying to soak up what I'd just seen when Honey lets out a mix between a squeal and a laugh. "Dan Wan! Long time no see, sugar."

A short man pivots on his heel, and as soon as he sees her, he starts running in place. Leather Bikini had nothing on Dan Wan's outfit. His dark hair is tipped light blonde and frozen upright in about a three inch faux hawk. He has streaks of sparkly iridescent glitter that extend from the corners of his eyes clear to his hair line. His pouty lips are painted robin's egg blue, and a dark streak of contour powder makes his cheeks look permanently sucked in. He wears a blue feather-trimmed bolero jacket, white leather booty shorts, and white thigh high boots. "Awwww, honeylicious! I could just spread you all over my toast and eat—you—up! Yes, I could. What are you doing my way, and who's this?" he asks, his tone suddenly dropping an octave. He eyes me curiously, and not in a very friendly way.

"This is Magnolia," Honey answers, and before she can continue, he interrupts.

"What kind of name is Magnolia?" He clicks his tongue for emphasis.

"What kind of name is Dan Wan?" I snidely retort.

He snaps his head my way, angrily sucking on his teeth. "You ever heard of Don Juan?"

"Of course," I answer.

"Well, Don Juan has nothing on Dan Wan, child. Tales of my loving have traveled the globe multiple times. I've been in the company of muscular men on the isles of Greece and charismatic businessmen in the Swiss Alps. I have left men speechless simply by entering the room, and I have rendered men unconscious with my insatiable sexual appetite. Can you say the same, baldie?"

"Dan Wan! Cut it out. She's my friend," Honey snaps. Dan quickly draws his hand to his lips.

"Are you... Oh, my. I thought you were trying to make a bold, yet very bad statement with that bald head of yours. I had no idea you were sick. Hundreds of apologies, dear. Keep up the good fight."

"She's not sick; she's a klutz," Honey says. "She burned her hair off by accident."

"Oh," Dan says mildly amused. "Well, I suppose I'll hold off on any comments I may have brewing in this fabulous head of mine since everyone is so touchy tonight. What can I help you with?" His question is loaded with attitude.

"I need someone to pop her cherry. I want to start easy, though," Honey answers.

"Ooooo. I need to think on that one." He draws his finger to his chin and taps it lightly.

"I don't want it to be him," I whisper, but Dan overhears me.

"Oh, don't you worry about that, cue ball. Dan Wan is strictly dickly. Just the thought of going," he waggles his forefinger up and down, "…there." He pretends to be overcome with nausea, and Honey gives him a swat across the shoulder.

"We get the point, princess. Quit being a bitch and answer the damned question."

He rolls his eyes. "I hear there's fresh meat working two blocks over and to the left. Word is that he's pretty new to the game, so you could probably work something out with him at a decent price."

"Now, was that so hard?" Honey asks.

"I know all about hard. *Rawr*!" he says, pawing at the air before giving his oversized package a conceited squeeze.

"Perv," Honey says.

"I learned from the best, love bug. Good luck with your deflowering, Uncle Fester."

Honey shoots him a disparaging look, but he laughs loudly while sashaying further down the alley. "I have a serious love-hate relationship with Dan Wan. His mom was one of my co-workers. She died young, so me and a few of the other girls did our best to look out for him while he grew up."

"That's quite a story. I'm not ready to lose my virginity tonight, Honey," I anxiously reply.

Honey stops walking and lets out a hearty laugh. "You're not gonna. You're just gonna experience your first make out session, and that's it. You're far from ready for anything else. Baby steps, Maggie.

Baby steps."

"Oh," I say, blowing out a sigh of relief. I quickly catch up to Honey, and together we stroll to the side street Dan Wan recommended. It's pretty empty except for one man leaning against a telephone pole and another further down who appears to be dancing, or perhaps warding off a swarm of bees?

"Just my opinion, but I'd say go with telephone pole guy. He's well dressed, looks pretty cute from here, and if what Dan says is true, you'll be able to negotiate with him a little." She slips a few bills into my hand. "Start with five dollars, but don't go over ten. A quick make out session shouldn't cost ya much."

"You're going to make me go down there by myself? I don't know what to say!" I assert excitedly.

"Shhh. He's looking this way. Keep your cool," Honey says, giving him a quick wave. He smiles back, and my knees go wobbly. He's not just cute; he's gorgeous. His dark hair is slightly mussed, but in an incredibly sexy way. He's wearing a button up shirt that accentuates his broad shoulders and tapers slightly at his waist. Dark jeans, a chunky gold pinky ring, and a confident grin complete his attire. "Oh, sugar, you're gonna enjoy this one. That man right there is fine with a capital F. Here's another ten. Pay it if he asks for it."

She pushes me toward him, but I slink back. "I don't know what to say," I whisper.

"Just tell him what you want from him. He's

looking. Go!" She pushes me again, but this time she makes a shooing motion with her hands when I look back. "Now," she mouths.

I nod and mouth back, "Okay!"

My heart is thudding in my chest as I approach him. He straightens up when he realizes I'm making my way in his direction. "Hi. How are you tonight?" he asks in a silky smooth voice. All I can do is giggle nervously. His smile grows broader. "You looking for a good time, sweetheart?"

I giggle some more. "Yes. Sort of. I'm sorry. I'm new at this. My friend suggested I do this because I'm not really all that experienced, and she thinks that paying someone will help me to gain some confidence."

With one step, he self-assuredly plants himself inches from my lips. "I'm here for you, baby. All we need to do is work out the technical stuff. You okay with paying?"

I nod. "Yep, she sent me with some money."

"Good. Good. Anything specific you wanna request before we set a price?"

"Tongue. She said I should make sure you know I want you to use your tongue."

"Ahhh, some oral gratification. I see," he says with a broad smile. "I'm an expert at that." He provocatively licks his lips, and I get the urge to pee my pants. "How much you got there, sweetheart?"

"She said I should start with five."

"Five. Five's fair, I suppose. How long do you

see this lasting?"

"Uh, maybe five or ten minutes?" I guess.

"Give me some credit now. Darlin, I can go all night for eight."

"I don't think I need all night. She said she just wants me to experience it this way first, and then I can move on to finding a real boyfriend."

"First? Like you mean you never?" he grins broadly. "Well, I must say that I'm flattered. Tell you what, I'll give it to you half off. Four, and I promise that I'll use lots and lots of tongue all night long." He leans in close enough to flick my earlobe with his tongue, and my breath catches in my chest.

"Yes. Four, okay. Do you have change?"

"Always," he breathes into my ear. "You know what else I have?"

"What?" I barely choke out.

"Handcuffs." I feel the cold steel bracelet brush up against my wrist, and by the time I fully register what's going on, my hands are secured behind me. "You're under arrest for solicitation of prostitution. You have the right to remain silent. Anything you say can and will be used against you in a court of law. You have the right to an attorney and to have him or her present with you while you're being questioned. If you can't afford one, one can be appointed to you before questioning if you'd like. You can exercise these rights anytime you wish. Do you understand your rights?"

"Wait. What? I didn't ask you to sleep with me!

You were only supposed to make out with me. That's not prostitution—is it? Did they change the definition of prostitution? What about people who run kissing booths? Are they illegal now?" I ask, spinning around to try to face him.

"Stay as you are," he says, pulling a neck badge from underneath his shirt so it hangs against his chest. Honey comes dashing up to us.

"What in the hell's going on?"

"Well, if it isn't Honey LeReaux. A little far from home, aren't you? Whatcha doing down on this end?"

"Fuckin' Nick. I didn't recognize you. I guess I need to invest in some glasses. Why is she under arrest? That girl ain't done a bad deed in her life."

"Well, there was that time I thought about…" Honey shoots me death daggers, so I censor myself.

"Give it a rest, Honey. I got everything I need to make the arrest. There isn't a person around that's going to pay someone four hundred dollars for a make out session."

I whip my head around. "Four *hundred* dollars! I thought you meant four dollars!"

"Four dollars? Lady, please. I don't have time for this nonsense."

"She's telling you the truth. Check her pockets to see how much money she's carrying."

"Any guns, needles, or weapons I should know about before I search you?" he asks.

"No." After swallowing a large gulp of air, I give

119

Honey a look of sheer terror.

"Well, I'm glad to see you're staying true to your name," Honey spews.

He stops emptying my pockets long enough to give her a derisive look. "Care to elaborate?"

"Nick the Dick. That's what everyone calls you. Even your co-workers."

He throws his head back as a hearty laugh escapes him. "You know what? They're right. Step out of your shoes please, ma'am," he directs at me.

"You'll have to unzip the boots for me. I can't just slide them off," I say.

"No funny business. Understand?" I nervously nod my head, and he stoops to make quick work of unzipping them. Once I kick them off, he gives Honey a wily smile. "Your story just fell to pieces." He holds up a few hundred dollar bills I have stuffed in my shoe. Honey glares at me.

"You took my twenty bucks, and you had hundreds stuffed in your boot?"

"I was gonna give it back to you," I say defensively.

"Even so, you have to know that she wasn't looking for no sex," Honey interjects.

"I told her I'd do her for four, and she accepted," Nick asserts.

"All she accepted was a make out session for four dollars, and now that I know who you are, I think that's about three dollars and seventy five cents too much," Honey says.

"How old are you? Late twenties, early thirties?" he looks my way. I nod. "And you seriously expect me to believe that in all those years you've never kissed anyone. Does it look like I have stupid written across my forehead, ladies? You two need to come up with better stories."

"It's the truth. I got to hear the whole pathetic story this evening," Honey pipes in.

"Honey! Feelings!" I say.

"Save it for the judge, you two. One-five-four, send in the unmarked," Nick says into his sleeve. When the police car stops in front of us, I lose it.

"No! I can't go to jail. Big Daddy's gonna kill me." I let out a high-pitched wail. "Please, Mister Dick. Please don't make me go to jail. I'll never ask anyone for a kiss again. I swear."

"The name's Nick, and it's out of my hands now. Who in the hell is Big Daddy?"

"Muh-muh-my father, Murray Berrybush."

"Whoa shit. Your dad is Murray Berrybush?" Nick asks in between laughs. "I love that dude. I know I shouldn't because he makes a living trying to get the scum we arrest off their charges, but damned if he doesn't make going to court fun. Please tell me your dad is going to represent you."

"I probably won't make it to court since he's going to kill me," I say in between sobs. "Please, please rethink this. I can't be arrested."

"You *are* arrested, now watch your head when getting in the car," he says.

"Gimme the money you had in your boot, and hopefully it'll be enough to spring you from jail," Honey requests.

Nick looks my way, and I nod my approval. He hands the bills over to her, and she disappears into the night. "Chances are you just lost that money."

"Honey wouldn't do that to me. She's my friend," I say, my sobs easing to sniffles.

"So how does the daughter of a notable lawyer end up being friends with a washed-up hooker from the projects? I think there's a pretty damned good story wrapped up in there, Ms. Berrybush. Magnolia," he says, eyeing my ID. "Seriously? Your name is Magnolia Picasso Berrybush? This isn't a fake?"

"No, it's not a fake! It's my name. You've picked on my inexperience, you've picked on my choice of friends, and now you're picking on my name. Anything else you'd like to belittle me about before bringing me in to ruin my life?"

"Darlin', you did the ruining. I did my job."

"I very strongly dislike you," I say with a huff.

"I wouldn't guess that with the way your knees buckled when I promised you lots of tongue." He closes the door, bangs on the roof, and blows me a kiss as the officer drives me to the station for processing. How can someone so unbelievably good-looking be so damned mean?

ten

"So I was able to scrounge up enough money to get ya out. I tried talking to the ADA, but it got me nowhere. They won't take the word of a working girl. I'm really sorry I got ya into this mess. I hope you know that my intentions were good," Honey claims as we're leaving the police station.

I'm given a court date two weeks away, so I figure it gives me a week and six days to come up with a plan to save my hide. If Honey was able to talk to the people in the district attorney's office, then maybe I can, too? If I go in calmly and tell them about the misunderstanding, maybe the charges can be dropped, and Big Daddy will be none the wiser. It's the hope that I'm going to cling to; the other option is far too scary to consider.

Honey offers to drop me off at home, but I remember my scooter in the cemetery. She goes home to rest, and I set off on foot to retrieve my wheels. Luckily, it's right where I left it, and better yet, it's full daylight so a lot of the creepy factor of being in a cemetery is gone. My intentions are to get some rest, as well, but despite the long, emotionally draining night and the super long walk, there's no way I'm going to sleep. Maybe a few laps around the park might clear my head and help me to relax some?

As near as I can tell, the park looks deserted, but after giving it a little thought, it only stands to reason that it should be. Six in the morning is pretty early for the kiddies to be swinging and sliding. Completely zoning out, I take a long stroll past the playground equipment and wind up on a paved jogging trail.

After following it for a few minutes, I'm suddenly aware that it's much darker, and I'm now in a thicket of trees. Crunching and popping sounds come from all around. Spinning quickly, I search for the source of the commotion, but I see nothing. My heart begins pounding in my chest, and my mouth goes dry.

The noises sound like they're coming from my right, then my left, then behind me. I grow dizzy from trying to track their source. Putting my head in my hands, I hope to regain my equilibrium. Instead, I'm knocked flat on my ass and left struggling for breath.

"Where did you come from? I'm so sorry! I was running, and thought I was alone... Magnolia?" the male voice asks.

I wipe away some of the tears that have welled in my eyes. "Jace?" I try to say. It sounds more like a raggedy exhale.

"Yeah, it's me," he says, squatting beside me. "Where does it hurt?"

"Everywhere," I answer, trying to get back on my feet.

"Whoa, whoa, whoa. Stay as you are until I'm sure you're okay. I used to play football, so I know how disorienting a solid hit can be."

Nodding, I allow myself to fall back onto my rear, and I carefully stretch out on the path under the trees. Jace looks on with concern, so I try to allay his fears. "I'm okay. I don't think you caused any permanent damage."

"You sure about that?" he asks. Damn, he looks good in his dark blue running shorts and white Nike t-shirt.

"Pretty sure."

He seems to accept the answer, and in an unexpected turn of events, he lies on the ground next to me. "Rough night?"

"Actually, yes. Why do you ask?"

"Lucky guess."

"Did you have a rough night, too?"

"Very," Jace answers.

"I'm sorry. Work?"

"Yep."

"Want to tell me about it?" I inquire.

He props up on an elbow. "I'll tell you mine if you tell me yours."

"I don't think that's a very fair trade off."

"Why not?" he asks with a slight chuckle. I give

125

him a half-hearted shoulder shrug. "That's okay. You don't have to tell me if you don't want to. Mine isn't all that interesting. We ran a bad call last night, and I find that going for a run helps with the stress."

"What happened?"

He puts his hands under his head and stares up at the tree tops where rays of sunlight are just starting to peep through. "A teenager died last night. It wasn't some unavoidable car accident or a chronic illness that he'd been battling all his life that killed him; it was stupidity. Instead of waking up and heading off to school, he's on a metal table getting reconstructed for his funeral while his family suffers from the grief of it all."

This time I prop up on my elbow. "That's terrible. Reconstructed?" I asked.

"That's what happens when you accept a dare to jump from the roof of one three-story building to another but misjudge the distance and pin ball off of obstacles all the way to the ground."

I begin to feel woozy, so I lie back down. "How terrible."

Jace rolls to look at me. "I'm sorry. I should've censored some of the details. If I'm discussing a call, it's usually with other medical personnel. I wasn't thinking."

"It's okay. I'm fine. I'm just sorry that you had to experience that."

"It's part of the job," he says. "Now, you tell me about your night."

I sit up and cross my legs then nervously pick through the twigs and leaves on the ground. Jace smiles at me. "That bad, huh? Come on. Tell me. You'll feel better. I feel better since I've told you about my night. What kind of wild mayhem went down?"

"How do you know that my night was wild? Maybe it was just long and boring."

"Just a guess. Plus, you only have one eyebrow drawn on your face. There has to be one hell of a story there." I reach up to touch my right brow bone. Jace shakes his head. "The other one."

I'm still not sure why I'm feeling around, there is nothing to touch but a thin layer of eye pencil. "I met a woman last night."

"Really? That's great. I hope you two are good for each other," Jace says with sincerity.

"What? Jace, I'm not gay. Not that there's anything wrong with being gay, but I'm attracted to men."

"But your apartment? The breasts everywhere? I thought you…"

"The boobs are my potentials. After I find a pair I like, I stick them up there for when I finally consult with a surgeon."

"Well, you've accumulated quite the collection there. Frat boys everywhere would be jealous of that boob wall."

I laugh loudly, startling myself when it comes forth. I toss my hand over my mouth. "I haven't done that in a long time."

"Hang hot knockers on your wall?"

I laugh again, and this time it feels less foreign. "No, silly. Laugh."

Jace's brows furrow. "Really? Come on. Not even for a TV show? Nothing has amused you recently? Not one tiny little thing?"

I shake my head.

"Well, that's a shame. You should definitely consider renting a comedy every now and again. Laughter is good for the soul."

"I'll start doing that," I say with a smile. I begin to sit up again, but Jace nudges me back down.

"Oh, no. You didn't finish telling me about your night."

Reluctantly, I close my eyes while telling him the story, as if my not being able to see him somehow makes me less visible. "The lady I met last night is a hooker named Honey, who despite her good intentions, helped me to get arrested for soliciting a male prostitute who turned out to be an undercover cop."

Jace is completely silent for about a minute. "Is there more to the story?"

"Oh yeah," I say. He breathes out a sigh. "I wasn't actually propositioning him for sex; he just misconstrued it as such."

Jace looks utterly confused. "What *were* you propositioning him for, Magnolia?"

A lump forms in my throat, and despite my best

efforts, my lower lip trembles. A tear slowly rolls down my cheek. "It was only supposed to be a kiss. I told Honey that I'd never been with a man before, and when she found out that included never having kissed a man before, she insisted on paying a male prostitute a few dollars to show me how it's done. The guy started talking numbers like four and eight. How was I supposed to know he was talking hundreds, not dollars? It was a big mess, and he turned out to be some undercover cop named Nick. I was hauled in to the station, booked, and let go this morning."

"Nick the Dick?" Jace asks.

I nod. "He a friend of yours?"

"Not exactly. I've run into him a few times on different calls. His nickname is fitting."

"He said there is no way he'd ever believe that a thirty-two year old woman had never been kissed, and he laughed when he found out who my father is. He's actually excited to see him in court. I don't even know if Big Daddy will defend me." Covering my face with my hands, I start to sob.

"Didn't you have a boyfriend when I picked up those patients from your house?" Jace queries.

"He was my boyfriend for a total of twenty minutes, and I don't think what he did was kissing."

"What did he do?" Jace asks with a smile.

"He kinda lapped at my face like a dog licking peanut butter from a spoon."

Jace roars with laughter. "No, that's not kissing."

"I knew you'd laugh at me. Ha! Ha! It's so

hilarious," I say with sarcasm.

Jace struggles with it a bit, but he finally grows serious. "I'm not laughing at you; I'm laughing at him. Although, like Nick, I'm finding it hard to believe that you've never been kissed."

"I used to look worse than this," I say.

"What are you talking about? Worse?"

"That day you found me in the art shop with my face smashed in, this is the before." I scroll through a few photos on my phone before I find the one I'd shared with Honey.

"And?" he asks.

"Look at me! My teeth are hideous, my nose is disgusting. I'm nothing but skin and bones..."

"Stop," Jace says. "It's obvious from the picture that you have some prominent features, but you know what stands out the most to me?"

"The teeth? They were repulsive."

"The dullness in your eyes."

"Seriously?" I ask, turning the phone so I can see the screen.

Jace rolls to a position where he can see my face. "Yes. It's as though I can see just how broken your spirit was. You may think that all of these things happening to you are negative, but they seem to have put a fire in your eyes that obviously wasn't there before."

"I wasn't expecting to hear that one," I say with an uncomfortable grimace.

"It's the truth."

I don't know what to say in response, so I quietly admire the view above.

"I could fix that for you if you want me to," Jace says after a minute or so.

"Fix what?"

"I could kiss you, and then you won't have to pay some stranger to do it."

My heart starts to flutter. "But your girlfriend..."

"I'm offering to give you your first kiss, not marry you, Magnolia. Besides, I'm in between girlfriends right now."

"But, that lady at urgent care was so pretty, and she seemed nice."

"She was, and still is, but we didn't click. That happens a lot with me. I don't generally date a person very long, and we're getting off topic. Do you want me to kiss you?"

My breathing begins to quicken, and my palms sweat. "I have *zero* experience when it comes to this stuff. Maybe it's best to leave it to a professional. I might be so bad at it that it could turn you off of women forever. Not to mention, I can't imagine making a bigger fool of myself than I've already done, but I know it's possible, so why take the chance, right?"

"Mags," Jace softly says while lightly palming the back of my neck.

"Yes," I eke out while gazing into his mesmerizing crystal blue eyes.

"Hush." His look says it all. He is calm, self-assured, and holy shit! He's going to kiss me! My inner teenager is squealing for joy, whilst my adult-self quivers uncontrollably. I'm incredibly thankful that we're still lying on the ground. "Don't be nervous," he whispers.

He edges closer and closer to me; his face so close to mine that I feel his breath on my lips. He gives a palpitation inducing grin as he closes his eyes, so I follow suit and close mine, too. His mouth melds with mine, his lips perfectly fitting into the ridges of mine. He softly strokes my lower lip with the tip of his tongue before firmly pressing it between them to part them. Once I open my mouth, he deepens the kiss. Sensations that I've never come close to imagining flood my senses, and I feel as though I'm floating. Kissing a living, breathing human is *nothing* like kissing a blow up doll. Jace pulls away slightly and after seeing the cockeyed grin on my face, tenderly leaves me with two more brief, yet powerful kisses before he sits up.

"Was that okay for a first kiss?" Jace asks with a smile.

I'm still not able to talk, so I simply nod.

"You remember what I did with my tongue?" he asks. Again, I nod. "It's not just a guy thing. You're free to experiment with that, too. It might feel awkward at first, but you'll get it. Come on. Try it once with me."

"No!" I squeak. "I mean, I can't. No."

"Wouldn't you prefer to try it out here with a

friend rather than in the midst of a hot date?"

"I don't really foresee any hot dates in my future, but I see the merit in your suggestion. Are you sure you don't mind?"

"Knock yourself out," he says, closing his eyes and puckering his lips. I laugh, so he opens them. "If you're good at this, I might touch your boob. It's just a habit." I give him a playful shove, and he laughs heartily. "Come on. Make my toes curl." He closes his eyes again, and though I'm still nervous, it's not nearly as bad as before. I do my best to emulate what he'd done with me, and then in a rare moment of bravery, I do a couple of things that feel natural to me. His hand leaves the back of my neck, and slowly drifts towards the front of my t-shirt. Once he has a handful of bra and breast, he gives a gentle squeeze, and I give him a firm swat. He laughs as he pulls away. "What?"

"You know what," I say with a smile.

"I figured we'd kill two birds with one stone. Now you can say you've gotten to second base. And to think, just five minutes ago, you'd never been kissed. You're making great strides pretty damned quickly, Magnolia Berrybush," he teases.

"Did I really do okay?" I ask, my voice laden with uncertainty.

"You did better than okay. You're quite good at it, actually. You have nothing to be nervous about the next time you kiss someone." He gives me a wink then stands up and brushes the dirt and leaves from the back of his running shorts before extending his hand to me. The familiar jolt sends shockwaves through my body as soon as our palms make contact, but I'm getting better at hiding it.

"Thank you for...you know—everything."

"Thank you for listening and for confiding in me. I hope I helped."

"Oh, you helped a lot," I say a lot more enthusiastically than I intend, and it earns me one of his killer smiles.

"You take care of yourself, Mags," Jace says, stretching briefly before jogging away. "Oh, one more thing..." he says, turning toward me as he jogs in place. "Don't pay a person for any of your firsts. You deserve much better than that." And with that final thought, he disappears down the trail. My fingers drift to my lips, and I can't help but smile. I feel more alive than ever! I want to sing, shout, and dance to celebrate the momentous event, but a quick shot of reality sobers me quickly. I still have to go home and tell my parents about the incident with Nick. Crap.

eleven

Big Daddy is nose deep in a newspaper when I come into the kitchen. There are voices coming from down the hallway, so I figure Sunny must be teaching class. I open the fridge to get a bottle of water before taking a seat across from Big Daddy at the table. It's his day off, so he's in the only other thing he wears besides his trademark seersucker suit, a track suit. I hear the fabric *swish* as he uncrosses his leg and plants his feet firmly on the ground.

"Is there something you'd like to discuss with me, Magnolia?" he asks without putting down the paper.

"Yes, sir. There is." *How does he know!* My stomach does a flip flop. I can't tell anything about his mood as long as he has that paper in front of his face.

"Interesting news today," he says, finally folding the paper and placing it on the table top. His fat finger slowly taps at an article close to the end of the page. I glance over to see what he's pointing out, and staring back at me in big, bold letters is my name. Slinking down in the seat, I cover my eyes with my hands.

"I was arrested, but wrongfully so. I never wanted sex from the guy."

"Hmmm. I see. Care to explain why you were in Merryland Heights at three in the morning talking to an undercover cop who just so happened to be posing as a male prostitute?"

"Not particularly," I say, hanging my head.

"Too bad." He rises from the chair so he can slip into full melodrama mode. After pushing out a long exhale, he heavily smacks his palm against the countertop. He points at me. "How can an undercover police officer possibly mistake your intentions if you were in the middle of a high crime neighborhood made famous by the sheer number of *whorehouses* encompassed in the area? If you weren't looking for sex, Magnolia, then what in God's name were you looking for?" He throws his hand skyward for effect.

"A kiss," I admit even though I'm humiliated. My answer throws Big Daddy off of his game because he takes a seat across from me.

"Did you say a kiss?" he asks in as soft of a voice as I've ever heard from him.

Refusing to look at him, I begin picking at my thumbnails. "I'm thirty-two years old, and until recently, I've never been kissed. I was curious about what it would be like, and a friend of mine suggested that I find out from someone with experience. Paying someone to kiss you isn't a crime. She told me I should offer him five dollars, but I could go as high as twenty dollars if need be. He totally misconstrued what I was asking for. I was talking dollars while he was talking hundreds of dollars, and even though I tried explaining to him what had happened, he insisted that I was lying and arrested me."

"Until recently?"

"Sir?" I ask.

"You said that you hadn't been kissed until recently. Did the undercover officer kiss you?"

I shake my head. There's no way I'm ruining my memory of Jace so I tell Big Daddy that it was some random guy from the park.

"Pity. I wish I had known you were so bad off, Magnolia. Sure you're introverted, but I had no idea that it's to the point that you don't live life. We desperately need to work on that. Desperate times call for desperate measures. You said something about a friend, right? The one who suggested that you hire a pair of lips. Are you two still friends?"

"I believe so," I reply, though I have no clue where this is going.

"Fine news. I want you to go stay with him or her."

"Her, and why?"

"Magnolia, the only way for you to truly experience life is to *live* it. That's not going to happen as long as you're holed up in that garage apartment. I've done you a huge disservice, and I intend to fix it. I'll represent you at your trial, but you must leave here effective immediately. Consider it a dose of long overdue tough love." My head is still reeling from the news when he walks into his office, and returns quickly with a stack of cash. "Here's seven hundred dollars to get you started. Offer your friend some rent money, and use some to buy yourself some clothes or whatever else you need. It is not to be spent on kisses or anything of the sort. Do you understand?"

"I can't believe you're kicking me out over this."

"I'm not kicking you out, Magnolia. I'm making you grow up." He kisses my forehead. "Call if you need money or advice." My mouth is still agape when he sits back down at the table and snaps open the paper.

"Am I allowed to pack a bag?" I ask.

"Sure. Take what you need, but make haste with it. No dawdling."

With a huff, I turn on my heel and stash the cash in the pocket of Honey's jeans that I'm still wearing from the previous night. There isn't really much for me to pack. All I have in my closet are articles that Honey forbade me to wear. I do, however, take down the boob wall and pack away all of the pornographic movies and sex toys. I also deflate the blow up man, and he tops the pile of boob pictures. Now that I've experienced intimacy, even though it was just a kiss, with a living, breathing human, I've garnered enough experience to know that there's no comparison. *Enjoy your retirement, Mr. Loverboy. Time for me to have a fresh start, and I'm gonna to try doing it the right way.* I make a final sweep around the garage apartment, but aside from my laptop, there is nothing I want or need.

It's close to three in the afternoon when I knock on Honey's door. I hear her hollering, but can barely make out what she's saying. "Hold your damned horses! Can't a person take a shit in peace?" The door flies open, and a startled Honey finishes drying her wet hands on her jeans. "Maggie, whatcha doin' here? I wasn't expectin' to see you again."

"Big Daddy kicked me out, and I have nowhere else to go," I say, choking back the tears.

She lets out a sigh. "Every bit of my being is telling me to send you packing, to tell you to go back home and plead with him to take you back, but seeing you standing here like a little lost puppy... Come on in. Where's your bag?"

"I don't have one. You said I'm not allowed to wear the skirts and turtlenecks anymore, I have no makeup, and all of my underwear is the kind you made fun of... Big Daddy gave me some money. He said I should give some of it to you if you let me stay. How much do you want?" I ask holding up the wad of cash.

"Okay. Put that junk away. We'll talk rent some other time. I don't usually hit the street until eight or so. Let me get my keys, and we'll find you something to wear."

"Oh, thank you, Honey!" I say throwing my arms around her neck. "Thank you. Thank you. Thank you! My life has been so much more exciting since meeting you. I thought the solicitation arrest was the end of the world, but it landed me a first kiss with the most amazing looking man! Is this how life usually works? A bad thing happens, but something good comes from it?"

"That ramble is missing some details, Maggie. What do you mean you were kissed? I was watching the entire time, and Nick the Dick never... Did something happen with him when you were behind bars?" Honey asks while unlocking the passenger door of the beast.

"No! He's so mean! No way. This guy is just as good looking, and he's a paramedic," I say with a squeal. The car struggles to start, but after a few tries, smoke infests the neighborhood, and it rumbles down the driveway.

"Tell me everything, because this story is making zero sense. A paramedic?"

"His name is Jace, and he's the guy who keeps showing up whenever I get hurt. Well, I wasn't ready to go home after getting released from jail, so I went to the park at the end of Beckingworth Drive, the one with the nice walking trail through the woods. I'm not paying attention to anything but my upcoming demise, and all of a sudden, I'm flat out on the ground. It was Jace. He smacked right into me because he wasn't paying attention either. I was stunned for a while, so he lay next to me on the ground, and we started to talk. He's real easy to talk to, and before I knew it I'd told him everything—about meeting you, the arrest, having never been kissed. He was really sweet about it, and he offered to kiss me for *free*!" I squeal.

"I'm assuming it was good?" Honey says with a smirk.

"Oh, it was sooooo good! His lips were soft, yet strong, and he was tender, but firm. It made my toes curl. Does that make sense?"

Honey laughs. "Yes. Yes, it does. It's nice to be around someone so excited about the things most people tend to take for granted. So what does this Jace guy look like?"

A goofy smile spreads across my face. "His hair is short and dark blond. He's tall, but not too tall. Maybe around six feet or so? But his eyes. Oh, my gosh! The most gorgeous shade of blue I've ever seen. And his smile. Makes me feel..." I bite my lower lip as I struggle to find the right word.

"Like you want to see him naked?" Honey asks.

"Exactly!" I shout. "But there's no way I could ever let him see me naked. Not that he'd ever want to, but..."

"Why do you say that? I saw you last night. Now that you've tidied up a bit, and once those battle wounds the razor left behind heal some, you have absolutely nothing to be ashamed of. Hell, if I had your body, I'd probably start stripping again."

My eyes grow wide, but I stay silent. There is no way in hell that I'll ever feel confident enough to take off my clothes in a room full of people.

"So, finish telling me about Jace," Honey prompts.

"There's not much more to tell. He kissed me and before he jogged off, he told me that I should never pay for any of my firsts."

"He said that?"

"Sure did."

"I like him," Honey says with a grin.

"That's good to know, but it doesn't really matter. He's so far out of my league that it's not even funny. Plus, he likes to date people in his profession. He told me so."

"You just never know..." Honey says as she parks the car in front of a thrift store. She turns sideways in her seat to face me. "Lookie. I could take you to the mall or some boutique and you can get maybe an outfit or two with what you have in your pocket, or you come with me in here and get about fifty outfits for two hundred bucks. The choice is yours, but if you want my opinion, I say we start here."

I nod, so Honey gives her door a swift kick to open it. Once we're inside, I'm amazed by the variety of clothing available. My previous wardrobe was all mail order, so seeing a plethora of choices in one place makes my head spin. Luckily, Honey is a pro at digging through the maze, and before I know it she's handing me a stack of clothes to try on. I feel completely intimidated and uncertain.

"Go. I'll bring you more as I find them," she says, shooing me towards the dressing room. I give the pile a wary look. There are short skirts, dresses, shorts—things I've never even considered wearing. She notices my hesitation and barks, "Go!"

Filled with diffidence, I slowly head to the dressing room. Honey picks up on my hesitation and tosses down the dress she has in her hand. "You're trying on clothes, not going in front of a firing squad. Give me those," she says, bustling toward me to snatch the pile from my arms. "You're trying this one on first." With the majority of the bundle in one hand, she starts throwing garments over her shoulder until she finds what she's looking for. "Here. Go put this on. If you don't like the way you look in it then we'll leave."

"You promise?" I ask, cautiously optimistic that the shopping trip might be over. As hard as I try, I can't fathom people enjoying this.

"Yep. Ain't no point in trying to help someone who don't want to be helped. I got plenty of other things I could be doing right now," Honey says, obviously miffed.

"I'm sorry, Honey. I'm being rude. Of course I appreciate your time and your advice. It's just that this is all new to me, and to be honest, it's pretty overwhelming."

Honey looks around the store, her face contorted into a look of disbelief. "What part of this is new to you?"

I stare down at my feet. "All of it."

"You're fucking kidding me, right? You're not seriously going to stand there and tell me that at thirty-something years old, *this* is your first time shopping for clothes."

"Until I was in my late teens, Sunny made my clothes. After that, everything came from…"

"Virgins Forever?"

"Ha. Ha. No, but they just showed up at my house once I ordered them. If they didn't fit, I sent them back and they mailed back the right size."

"These catalogs that you looked through for clothes, their only options were the crap you wore?"

"It's what I like. People didn't even give me a second look when I wore those clothes."

"And that's good?"

"It is if you're protecting yourself from the insults of the people who do notice." I plunk down on the chair next to the dressing room and put my face in my hands. Damn it if I don't start to cry. Honey sets the clothes down beside the chair and softly rubs my back.

"Hey, I didn't mean to upset you. I'm too abrasive. It's one of my faults. You have to ignore most of what I say."

I shake my head. "It's not you. I've never admitted the things I'm telling you to anyone. I did my best to pretend that the comments didn't bother me, or that I didn't hear them, but I heard them and they bothered me terribly. In school, I tried being the funny girl, the sweet girl, the hell raiser—no matter which persona I put out there, the teasing and picking never stopped.

Finally, I realized that if I stayed in the shadows, I was left alone. Life was better because I wasn't constantly getting hurt, but over thirty years have passed me by. I've missed out on so much because I was scared to stand up to people and say, 'Yeah, I have buck teeth and I'm flat as a board, but so what!' No school dances, no first date, no going shopping with the girls…" I suck in a shaky breath. "No slumber parties or *any* parties for that matter.

"Maggie, I had no clue it was this bad. Not to worry. You stay here." She shifts the pile of clothes to the checkout counter where the cashier begins to ring up the merchandise. Honey summons me with her finger, so I dry the tears from my eyes and meet her at the register. Once we load the bags into the car, Honey drives us to a drug store. "I'll need about sixty bucks, okay?" she asks.

I hand over the money without question or hesitation. She slams the door of the car once she gets out and gives it a solid kick to make sure the door is latched. Honey is definitely not someone to play around with. I admire her spunk. Maybe if I hang around her long enough, some of it will rub off on me. I can stand to gain some gumption.

She exits with a bag around each wrist and a bottle of wine in each hand. I push her door open for her, and she hands me the loot. "What's all of this?" I ask.

"The essentials for a slumber party. We're not going to play around with the kiddie telling- ghost-stories-in-the-dark bullshit. No ma'am. We're going to fast forward to the high school years when you experiment with makeup, try on different clothes, talk about boys, and steal from your parents' liquor cabinet."

"What?"

"Look, you're not the only person deprived of a childhood. Remember what I was doing at seventeen? I'm taking the night off, and we're going to act like kids. You're going to your first slumber party."

It's odd that a grown woman should get excitement from such trivial news, but my insides feel energized. A huge smile breaks across my face.

****

Honey stumbles from the kitchen, a soup spoon hanging from the corner of her mouth and a pint of ice cream in hand. She plops onto the sofa, plucks the spoon free, and points it at me. "You're doing that wrong. Wipe it off and try again," she semi-slurs.

Seated on the floor beside a coffee table laden with an arsenal of products, I pull back from the lighted mirror to see that I have mascara everywhere

BUT on my lashes. Letting out a frustrated sigh, I reach for the cold cream and tissues so I can once again start with a blank canvas. "I don't understand why this is so hard. You make it look easy."

"I've had lots of practice. Don't sweat it; you'll get there."

"I'm not so sure," I say, trying to decide which tube to pull from the makeup pile first.

"This one," Honey says. She leans forward to retrieve a permanent marker from the drawer of the shoddy end table to her left and begins to number the products for me. The spoon is once again hanging from the side of her mouth. She gives it a swirl with her tongue then plops it into the nearly empty tub of ice cream. "There. It's like paint by number. Start with number one and keep going until you run out of numbers."

I eye her curiously.

"What?" she asks.

"It's nothing. I shouldn't ask. It's embarrassing and rude…"

"Well, being that I don't get embarrassed, I think you should ask your question."

I nervously pick at the label on the blush compact. "That thing you did with the spoon. I've seen it before in movies. I was wondering…"

Honey thinks about it for a second before giving me a knowing smile. "You're curious about sucking dick?"

Still not used to Honey's candor, I plop my

forehead onto the coffee table. "Maybe. I guess. A little bit," I say, refusing to look her way.

"Well, being that you can't even look at me while talking about it, I doubt it's something you'll be attempting in the near future. Just be firm, in charge, and watch your teeth. Teeth are bad. Other than that, you can practice your swirling technique on suckers, candies—anything. I could give you step by step directions, but I think it's best we save that for when you become more experienced. Stick with makeup application for now. Don't want you going into information overload."

I take the compact marked *2* and begin to apply it to my face. "Have you ever been in love, Honey?"

She's topping off her wine glass, and as soon as the question escapes my lips, she swigs directly from the bottle. She tosses it over her shoulder, and it lands with a *kathunk* on the vinyl floor. "Yep. Once." The memory is obviously painful, so I quickly scramble to explain my line of questioning.

"I just heard that sex with someone you love is different from… Well, I was curious to know if it was true."

She gazes off into the distance. "It is. Very different." A smile crosses her lips. "But that was a lifetime ago."

"Will you tell me about it?" I inquire.

"There's not much to tell. I'd been hooking for a few years. I was at my high dollar prime, so my clients were elite businessmen for the most part. I fell for one, and I fell hard. He promised to take me away from the life. Told me he was in an unhappy marriage and couldn't wait to get out of it so we could be together."

"What happened?"

"He was a fucking liar, that's what happened. It was going to be like one of those romantic movies you see on TV. I was supposed to meet him at the airport for a six o'clock flight to the Bahamas. We were going to stay there for a few weeks to discuss where we wanted to go and what we wanted to do next. I showed; he didn't. End of story."

"Do you know what happened to him?"

"Don't know. Don't care."

"Maybe he ran a little late? What if you just missed him?"

She let out an inebriated huff. "I sat in that terminal until six the following evening. That's when security suggested I leave. I hopped a bus from New Orleans to Baton Rouge and been here ever since."

"What if he was looking for you? What if he was in an accident and couldn't make it? What if..."

Honey throws up her hand to stop my line of questioning. "What ifs will only drive you crazy. *If* he wanted to find me, he was in a position that he could have easily done so. *If* he was killed in an accident, then it's obvious we weren't meant to be together. I moved on and never looked back."

I look to the floor.

"Mags, romance is a great notion, but it's

nothing like what you see in the movies. TV and movie people have writers whose sole intention is to wrap up the stories in neat little packages with pretty little bows. The real world is nothing like that. Same goes for the pornos, sweetie. The pizza man isn't going to deliver a ten inch penis and multiple orgasms. It doesn't happen like that. They're meant to be reality escapes, not how-to guides. The sooner you realize that, the better off you'll be."

I feel a lump forming in my throat. "For thirty-two years, I've relied on the TV for everything, and now you're telling me that it's all lies. I don't think I've ever been more terrified of living than I am right now." My insides swell with panic. "Why am I feeling so intimidated all of sudden? I can't go out there! I was crazy to think I could do this! I need to plead with Big Daddy to take me back in. I need to go back to my garage apartment! I can't stay here. I can't... I can't... I. Can't. Breathe," I gasp.

Honey takes my face between her palms, looks me squarely in the eye, and then rears back to give me a solid slap on the cheek. "Snap out of it. You're freaking for no good reason. I said life's not like the movies, not that it isn't worth living. Damn, girl. Get a grip."

"You hit me," I sputter.

"I did, and you're not babbling like a fool anymore. You're welcome."

Rubbing my cheek, I shoot her a look. "I never said thank you."

She pulls the half empty wine glass she's chugging from away from her lips to place it on the end table. Red liquid sloshes onto her hand, and she rapidly laps it up before turning her attention back to me. "So you'll thank me later. Whatever. I think you should lemme fix your face up real nice. Member how perty it was the first day we met? Gorgeous. I'll show you how to do that. Now pay attention to what I do."

She slurs her speech; however, I think she's probably just slightly tipsy. My inebriation scale is obviously *way* off because she bursts into peals of laughter when the mascara wand she's holding rolls across my eyeball instead of my eyelashes.

"It hurts! It hurts! Oh, my gosh, it hurts so bad!" I scream, covering the injured eye while doing a jig.

"Oh, come over here so I can see, you big baby," she lisps. I refuse, so she charges at me like a raging bull. Once I land flat on my ass, Honey clumsily straddles me while trying to pry my hand from my eye.

"Get off! Now my back hurts, too. What's wrong with you?" I squirm as much as I can with Honey on top of me, but I get nowhere.

"Let. Me. See!"

I stop resisting at the same time she bears down to pull with all her strength. The end result is Honey, blood trickling from her rapidly swelling and slightly askew nose, out cold on the floor. Honey is making gurgling sounds, and I manage to call for an ambulance. It arrives in less than ten minutes, and of course, Jace is the first person through the door. He finds me sitting across from Honey, my head tucked between my knees as I draw long, slow breaths.

"Did someone call for... Magnolia? What happened? What are you doing here?" he says, dropping to his knee beside the unconscious Honey.

"Big Daddy kicked me out, so I live here now. We were fighting over mascara, and I accidentally knocked her out. Then came the blood. I got woozy, but I didn't faint this time."

Jace looked startled. "You knocked her out? Who knew you were such a bad ass? Is that why you're covering your eye? What were you fighting about?" he inquires while assessing Honey.

"Nothing. It wasn't like a fight fight; it was an accidental fight."

Jace blankly stares with those crystal blue eyes of his. "Thanks for clearing that up."

"You two know each other?" Jace's partner questions.

"Sort of," he answers.

I feel compelled to further explain the situation. "She had been drinking, and she wanted to show me how to put on makeup. The mascara got in my eye, and it burned like fire, so I went nuts. She wanted to see my eye, but I wouldn't let her. She tackled me, pulled on my arm, and knocked herself out."

Jace looks to his partner. "You take over here?" he asks. His partner nods and finishes strapping

Honey to the stretcher while Jace approaches me.
"Let me see your eye," he requests softly. He reaches
out to pull my hand from my eye, but like with
Honey, I resist.

Jace slowly shakes his head from side to side.
"Don't fight me. I'm not walking out of here with a
crooked nose. Relax. I'm not going to hurt you. Let
me see, okay." His voice is so incredibly soothing.
My stomach begins to do back flips. I slowly lower
my hand, and Jace touches the puffy orbital area with
his fingertips.

"Is it bad?" I cautiously inquire.

"Terrible. Half of your eyeball is missing and the
other half is painted black."

"Liar," I say, giving him a playful shove. I'm
amazed by how rock-hard his chest feels against my
touch. Trying to divert attention away from my
embarrassment, I re-cover my eye with my hand.

Jace gives one of his famous grins and reaches in
his medic bag to pull out some supplies. He gently
pads and bandages my eye. In my mind, the moment
is sweet and intimate. In reality, it's probably nothing
of the sort. Honey is still out when the guys load her
into the back of the ambulance. Jace's partner climbs
in the back with Honey, while Jace insists that I ride
up front in the cab with him.

"Are you going to put on the lights?" I excitedly
ask while rapidly taking in the myriad of buttons,
lights, and equipment littering the dash.

"No," Jace answers. "I need you to put on your

seatbelt."

Once I'm clicked in, he says some gibberish into the microphone and puts the ambulance into gear. We slowly coast down the deserted street.

"Are you the only medic for this company or something?" I ask. "You always show up."

"I'm sure it's mostly coincidence, but I do work more shifts than the others."

"Why?" I ask.

"I just like picking up extra shifts, I guess." I can tell from the look on his face that the line of questioning is making him uncomfortable, so I let it drop.

"What about you? Why are you living in the worst part of town with whom I assume is Honey the hooker?"

"I told you. Big Daddy kicked me out. He said the only way to experience life is to go out and live it. I had nowhere else to go."

"And the charges against you? Any word on a court date?"

"Two days. Big Daddy says the sooner we get this over with the better."

"Well, Mags, your life is far from boring," Jace proclaims.

"I've never thought of it that way. Unfortunately, it's not really positive things that are keeping the excitement alive."

"No?" Jace asks. "Not one positive thing in the whole messy mix?"

I know he's hinting about the kiss, and my cheeks turn crimson. "Maybe one positive," I say nervously.

"How positive?" Jace teases.

"You're embarrassing me!" I fuss, anxiously gnawing at my thumbnail while looking out the passenger window. "It was the most positive thing to ever happen to me," I spit out before losing the nerve. I'm not sure what his reaction is because I refuse to look his way, and he remains silent until we reach the hospital.

Honey's awake when they pull her from the back of the ambulance. "What the fuck happened? Where am I? Why is the world spinning so fast? I feel…" She projectile vomited right on the ER ramp.

"It's the hospital's problem once the patient's out of the ambulance," Jace's partner points out while stepping over the puddle. Jace and his partner have to leave the hospital quickly because of another emergency call, so Honey is put in one room, and I'm escorted to another by an admin clerk. A couple of hours later, each sporting fresh bandages, we meet in the waiting room.

"What'd they tell you?" Honey asks.

"Minor scratch. Eye drops three times a day. The eye patch is temporary, but the puffiness might last a bit. You?"

"He set my nose and said I can expect black eyes and to keep this splint thingy in place for a couple of days." With my one good eye, I try to convey sympathy. I don't think it works. "What's wrong with you? Are you trying to fall asleep on me or something?" Honey asks. Nope, the sympathetic look doesn't work with just one eye.

"No, I'm not falling asleep on you. I know what it's like to wear one of those nasal splints, though. I'm sorry."

"Eh, it is what it is. Good thing some of my regulars are scheduled the next couple of days. No need for me to try to solicit business on the streets. No telling what kind of pervs a beat up face will draw in. Come on. Let's head back to my house. I'm wiped."

"Agreed, but how do we get home?"

Honey gives me a look. "You seriously have no clue of how to survive in this world. Zero. Zilch. Nada."

I'm not sure whether or not to be offended.

"We're going to call a cab to take us home. Come on and pay attention. You don't know if you'll need to do this for yourself sometime in the future," she says, shaking her head as she walks down the hall.

Big Daddy asks me to meet him at the courthouse for eight o'clock. I'm on time; he's not. I take a seat just outside the courtroom on a long empty wooden bench that lines the corridor. I nervously run my hands through my hair, which is finally long enough to lie semi-flat. Honey says it looks like a pixie cut, and that my short dark hair makes my green eyes pop. I'm still not sure about it. She also suggested my wardrobe, a white and green dress that came with a bolero jacket. She wanted me to wear heels with it, but I know better. I need lots more practice before donning heels in public. I have on no makeup, first because I wasn't sure how much to use, and second, because my eye is still pretty darned puffy and crusty. It's embarrassing, but Big Daddy said that a crusty eye wasn't reason enough to reschedule the trial.

Honey wanted to be with me, but I let her sleep because her late night visitor didn't leave until the wee hours of the morning. He tried to sneak by the sofa I was resting on, but his patent leather shoes made this funny squeak/fart sound that prevented a quiet exit. He departed around five, so I didn't dare wake Honey for this.

My head is in my hands when I feel someone sit beside me. I slowly straighten, and I'm dismayed to see Nick the Dick dressed in a perfectly pressed uniform and sporting a shit-eating grin that rivals the Cheshire cat's. He looks beyond handsome now that I get the chance to see him in the daytime, and I begin to feel the butterflies fluttering in my stomach—until he opens his mouth.

"What happened to your eye? Catch some kind of cooties from your hooker friend?" he asks.

"That's just mean, and totally uncalled for. If you must know, I hurt my eye while trying to figure out how to use mascara. Isn't it illegal for you to harass me before the trial or something?"

"I asked a question about your well-being. That's not harassment; that's courtesy."

"I have enough going on today without your *courtesy*. Feel free to find someone else to inquire about." A loud ruckus echoes down the corridor as Big Daddy heaves his girth through one of the double doors at the end of the hall. He has his briefcase and several large posters under one arm, and a cup of coffee with a donut precariously balanced atop in the other.

"Daughter, please come help Big Daddy with his

things," he requests, and I instantly jump up to take some of the load from his arms. I'm on the verge of tears when I realize that the posters are huge, blown up headshots of me before my facial surgery.

"What are these for?" I ask, choking back the emotions racing through my body.

"This, my dear, will help to prove to the judge that your 'never been kissed' story holds water. One look at these and it's likely he'll find it absolutely plausible that you were merely searching for legalized affection."

"So, you plan to humiliate me to win the case?" I ask.

"Would you prefer to sit behind bars for a few months?"

"No, Big Daddy," I say, hanging my head.

"Darlin', you know Big Daddy's gonna do whatever he's got to, and if you have to suffer through a few minutes of embarrassment, I think it's a small price to pay."

"Yes, Big Daddy," I half-heartedly agree.

"Good girl," he says, taking a bite from his donut and a gulp from his coffee. "Have a seat out here for a minute. I'm going to have a talk with the judge for a bit." With that, he disappears through a heavy wooden door that has a placard stating "Do Not Enter."

I plop back onto the bench and angrily toss the posters beside me. Nick nabs one, and eyes it carefully. "Who's this?" he asks after a beat.

I turn to face him. "Who the hell do you think it is? It's me. You don't have to make any of your sick jokes or your rude comments about how ugly I am. My father will be doing it in front of a packed courtroom, so you can save your breath."

"Why do you look so different now?"

"My face was reconstructed after an accident," I answer with tears welling in the corners of my eyes. Not wanting to give Nick the satisfaction of seeing me cry, I quickly dash them away to stare out of the window across the hall. It's not long before he's standing behind me. I feel his hand on my shoulder, and it takes him hardly any effort to spin me around to face him. He's holding one of the posters in his other hand, and he looks from it to me several times before he speaks.

"I want you to look me in the eye. No bullshit; no lies. Is this you?"

"Yes," I answer. "That picture was taken about six months ago."

"And in your entire life, you've never been kissed? Ever?"

"I thought I had once, but it turns out he was just licking my face. I finally had a first kiss, but it didn't happen until after you arrested me."

His eyes rapidly dart back and forth as they search mine for the truth. "How is that possible?"

"I don't know. Look at the picture. Isn't that answer enough to your question?"

"You look a little… But seriously. Not one

person."

"Would you like for me to take a polygraph? No. No one."

He shakes his head from side to side as he strolls off mumbling to himself. He comes back to stand before me. "Do you know what sex is?"

"I'm ugly, not stupid," I snap.

"No, Magnolia. You're far from ugly. The crusty eye isn't all that attractive, but you have lots of potential beauty. You really should quit being so hard on yourself."

"Whatever," I say, turning away from him.

"Stay here. I'm going to find the DA. I believe you, Magnolia, and if I can convince him that your story is legit, maybe he'll drop the charges."

"Really?" I asked, suddenly perking up.

"No promises. I'm only agreeing to talk to him." I throw my arms around his neck and hug him so tightly he can barely talk. "Okay, that's enough. For goodness sakes, let go. I have a reputation to uphold. Can't let people know that I'm secretly a softie." He gives me a quick wink before disappearing behind the same door that Big Daddy went through. After about ten minutes, he pops out long enough to grab one of the posters then ducks back inside the door. The next time I see him, my fingernails are chewed to nubs. Big Daddy is right behind him, a huge grin plastered on his face.

"You're free to go home, Magnolia. The charges have been dropped, but you're forbidden from frequenting that part of town again. Do you understand?"

"Yes, sir. Thank you."

"The thanks go to Sergeant Ferrera," Big Daddy corrects.

"Thank you, Sergeant Ferrera," I say, shyly.

"You're welcome, Magnolia. I believe your story, and despite the fact that you're living with a known prostitute, you've been given a second chance. Don't make me regret it."

"You won't. I really want to hug you, but I know you don't like that, so would a handshake be okay?"

Nick gave a sort of half-smile that left my knees wobbly. "A handshake is fine." I thrust my hand out towards his, and in a move that astounds me, he twists it to place a gentle kiss on the top of my hand. "Take care, Magnolia."

I'm still stumbling for words when he walks away. As I watch him strut confidently down the hall, I get the overwhelming urge to do to him some of the things I'd seen in the porn movies I used to watch. I fantasize about ripping his shirt open to expose his hard, chiseled chest, and a shudder runs through my body. Deciding to save the rest of the fantasy for later that night, I rejoin Big Daddy at the end of the hall.

He tells me that he'll be returning to his office to tie up a few loose ends, and then he and Sunny are off to Key West. Nice to know he was so confident that the trial would go well! Or, maybe he didn't really give a patoot if I was cleared or locked up? Either way, it's over, and I'm suddenly exhausted. I call a cab to bring me back to Honey's, and then I sleep for the rest of the day. Well, I sleep until Honey decides it's time for me to wake up.

"What happened? Why didn't you wake me up! I wanted to be there with you. Are you okay? Tell me!"

I slowly edge my way upright and let out a huge yawn while rubbing my eye. By doing so, I notice that the puffiness is gone from my eye. Honey must notice too because she comments about it.

"Well, you're back to normal. But me, I still have a few days to go," she says in reference to the raccoon eyes she's sporting. "Anyway, stop with the suspense! What happened in court today?"

"Nick isn't such a dick, although he doesn't want others to know it. We talked for a little while before court, and he realized that it was all a big mix up. He believed that I was telling the truth, so he talked to the DA and the charges were dropped. I can't go back to that part of town, but I'm good with that. It's not like I went there often anyway."

"The assholiest of all asshole cops promises to make a mockery out of you, then after a brief conversation before your trial is set to begin, he argues to get your charges dropped? Why does that sound fishy to me?"

"I don't know." I shrug. "Big Daddy was planning to humiliate me to win the case. He had these huge headshot posters of the old me blown up to put around the courtroom. Nick saw them and the conversation went on from there."

"And you were told that the charges were dropped. Not that you accepted a plea? No probabtion? Nothing?"

"Nope. It wasn't a plea; the case was dropped."

"Well, slap my ass and call me Sally! We need to celebrate! I'm going to dress you up and take you out!" I give her a wary look. "Don't worry! I'm sober this time. I can't wait to doll you up! Let's go pick something for you to wear, and then I'm gonna do your nails. After that, you'll hop in the shower, and I'll do up your hair and makeup. It's gonna be so much fun!"

My enthusiasm is nowhere near Honey's level, but I feign it for her benefit. She tosses outfits around until she comes across something she says all women must have, a little black dress. I try it on, and I have to admit that I like what it does to my body. The hem comes about mid-thigh, which makes my legs look extra-long. Between the extra boobage I've gained and the hips I've acquired, the dress accentuates my new hourglass figure. It's a far cry from the stick figure I used to be, and I can't help but smile at my reflection. I have boobs! Pretty boobs! My hands instinctively rise to grope them, and Honey laughs. "Still not used to the girls yet, huh?"

"Not really. Is it wrong for me to like having them so much?"

Honey laughs. "No. Nothing wrong with that at

all. They make a lot of men go gaga. They want to touch 'em, squeeze 'em, lick 'em, suck 'em, even fuck 'em. You just don't go letting anyone have their way with you or make you do something you're uncomfortable with, no matter how much he might beg. Understand?"

I'm still trying to process everything she'd told me about breasts, but I manage to nod my head and this makes her happy. She leaves the room for a second and returns with a mini nail salon. She gives me more pointers about sex and how men will act around me. She also tells me what to look out for, and how to get out of awkward or uncomfortable situations.

"You're not going to send me in there alone, are you?" I ask, my mouth suddenly dry.

"No! We're going together, but what if you get asked to dance? I can't very well stand beside you to give advice. You're gonna have to learn how to interact on your own. Unfortunately, you're starting the game a little late, but it's okay. I'm gonna keep a close eye on you until I'm sure you can handle yourself."

Making sure I don't smudge my nails, I lean in to give her a monster hug. "Thank you for everything you've done and continue to do for me, Honey. I owe you so much."

Honey shrugs it off. "Says who? I'll be honest; you helping me as much as I'm helping you. I been lonely for a long time, Magnolia. I might have company in my bed every night, but those guys don't give a rat's ass about my feelings. They don't want to have dinner with me. They don't want to be seen in public with me, and they definitely don't want to hear how my day went. You the first friend I had in a long time."

"You're the first friend I've had—ever!" I say with a laugh.

"But I won't be your last. You come a long way, and I see a lotta good things in your future. Now, let's go find a wig for you to wear. I like your hair short, but I think it's time to change it up a little bit."

I follow her into her bedroom where she helps me into a long, dark wavy wig. She refuses to let me see myself in the mirror until she's finished with me, and that means makeup, jewelry, even shoes. She makes me promise to keep my eyes closed, which I do, as she positions me in front of the full length mirror.

"Okay, open in three, two, one," she says.

I want to cry when I see the person staring back at me, but I know it'll ruin the makeup Honey spent so much time applying. The wig looks completely natural, with long dark brown curls that shine deeply in the light. Smoky black shadow accentuates my eyes, making them glimmer like huge emeralds. Just a hint of rosy blush gives my skin a healthy glow, and the nude color Honey picked for my lips makes them appear full and plump.

The dress, combined with the sexy undergarments that Honey insists I wear, gives my body more shape.

Just the right amount of cleavage shows from the V-neck of the dress, and though the dress clings to me provocatively, it's not too tight. Honey spends a lot of time debating about which shoes I should wear, and she decides it will be best for me to wear a pair of strappy sandals with thick heels, even though "stilettos woulda killed it."

I'm still staring at my reflection when she comes out of the bathroom dressed in a royal blue spandex number complete with mesh cut outs. It's a little more revealing than I'd be comfortable with, but it looks good on her, especially with me knowing her age. She pushes me away from the mirror so she can adjust herself in the dress. "Every night's a work night for me," she says with a grin and a shrug.

"I understand," I assure her, even though I feel sad that this is her life.

"Good. Let's go celebrate! And don't worry. I'm not taking you to any of the seedy joints. Oh no! You're looking way too good for those dives. We're going to a real club; we're going to the casino."

That isn't what I'm expecting to hear. I scrunch my brows. "The casino?"

"Well, yeah. You know the men there have money. There's a night club inside to do your dancing and such, then you can also break away from it for a while and mingle among the gamers. It's the perfect place."

"If you say so," I reply. "I'm just going for the ride."

A horn beeps from outside, and Honey checks the window. "Cab's here. Let's go have some fun!" She dances her way out the door.

I'm nervous, excited, and hesitant at the same time, but I follow Honey's lead. Before I know it, I'm standing at the gang plank of a massive floating casino. I'm in awe of the bright lights at the rich, elegant entrance, but Honey leaves me little time to appreciate it all. She grabs my hand and practically pulls me up the carpeted ramp. The outside is nothing compared to the inside. Machines bing, sing, and call from all around me. Lights flash in all different colors of the rainbow, and people dressed in porter style uniforms disappear and reappear in the crowds of people. Some of the guests are wearing full out regalia, tuxes and ball gowns, while others sit around in sweat suits and flip flops.

"Is this for real?" I ask, drinking in the sights around me. Honey shakes her head and laughs.

"Come on. The club's this way." We go up an escalator and down a blue-lit hallway. A pair of blacked out double doors, manned by a burly guy wearing a suit, stands at the end. As soon as we get close enough, the man opens the door for us and music blares into the hall.

"Ladies. Looking nice. Have a great night," he says as we pass through the doors.

"Thank you," I mutter with a timid smile. It earns me a wink.

Once inside, we take a minute to assess the room,

and Honey decides that a trip to the bar should be our first stop. She insists on buying me a drink, but I'm hesitant after seeing what happened to her after two bottles of wine. She assures me that one drink isn't going to send me over the edge, and if anything, it will help me to relax. Whatever it is she gives me, it's sweet and creamy, so I suck it down in no time. Warmth fills my insides, and within minutes, I'm feeling ready to conquer the world.

"What do we do now?" I yell over the music.

"I'm going to talk to that guy over there for a minute. He's an old client. You stay here. Get yourself a soda or another drink or something."

"What is it that I just drank?"

"White Russian," she yells.

"It was yummy."

"Don't drink too many, too fast. They'll sneak up on ya," she advises before walking off.

"I have to say, she gives good advice. White Russian for the lady please," Nick says to the bartender. I freeze. First, I had no idea he was sitting beside me, and second, well, it's freaking Nick!

"She does. You shouldn't knock her for her profession," I say in a slightly scolding tone.

"You know what I do for a living, right? Prostitution is kind of frowned upon in the eyes of the law."

"It's her only income."

"It's illegal."

"I'm not here to argue with you," I say, smiling at

169

the bartender as he deposits my drink in front of me. Nick pays and asks for another beer. It's in front of him in no time flat.

"What are you here for? Learning the business? You look really nice, by the way."

"You insult and compliment me in the same breath. Wow."

"It wasn't an insult. It's an honest question."

"No, I have no desire to learn Honey's business, and I'm sorry she's in a position that she has to support herself that way. I don't look down upon her; I feel bad for her. So, no, I'm not in training to be a prostitute. Besides, I'm nowhere near ready for that kind of thing. I only had my first kiss about a week ago."

"You're still sticking with that story?" he quips.

"It's the truth, and you said you believed me this morning. That's why you had the charges dropped. Why are you giving me grief now?"

He slides back in his chair and raises his hand to point at me. "*This* does not look like a woman who has just had her first kiss. *This* looks like a sex goddess ready to turn the hearts of men into mush."

His words affect me so much that I start to tremble. "No one has ever said anything like that to me before." I take a deep breath then look him in the eye. "You have no reason to lie to me, do you? You really think that I look…"

His eyes narrow. "Sometimes I think you're toying with me, and others, I think you're being sincere. I've never met anyone like you, Magnolia. You throw me off my game, and I'm not sure that I like it. But, damned if I can't help but be intrigued by you. And to answer your question, yes, I really think you look incredible tonight."

I think my heart stops beating. My first ever compliment on my appearance and it comes from an asshole who is known for his candor. I feel like I'm floating, and I'm somewhat embarrassed that this handsome dickhead is making me feel this way.

"Thank you," I manage to eke out in between sips from my glass.

"Have you ever danced before?" Nick asks over the ballad that's playing.

I shake my head. He removes the drink from my hand and pulls me to the dance floor. "We're going to take care of that right now," he says, confidently snaking one hand around my waist.

"But I don't know how…"

He presses a finger to my lips. A jolt shoots through me. "Shhh. I'm going to show you. Listen to the music. Hear the beat? I'm going to lead, and you're going to follow. I'm going to pull you close to me, and we're going to sway back and forth in time to the music. Okay?" he asks.

I nod, and he pulls me in so closely that my nose rests at the base of his neck. He smells delicious! My instincts tell me to lick him, but my mind knows it's wrong. His hips begin to rock, so I move mine in sync with his, and though it's somewhat awkward at first, I catch on quickly. Once my brain goes into "dance autopilot," panic starts to set in. My body is suddenly very aware that I'm mashed up against an Adonis of a man, and weird things start to happen. My heart rate picks up, my breathing feels labored, and I think my palms are sweating! *Oh, my God his shoulders are broad!* Weird things happen south of the border. My hooha has never tingled before, but it's flocked with energy tonight. I try to make sense of it all, but I can't.

Nick must sense my unease, and he pulls away slightly to cup my face in his palms. "You're doing fine. Don't tense up. Relax," he calmly requests. His voice melts me, and I'm happy to enjoy the sensation of close, personal human contact. The song is over much too quickly, and Nick escorts me back to the bar. I reach for my drink, and I'm about to take a huge swallow when Nick pulls it from me.

"You have so much to learn. You can't drink that. Never drink from a glass or open bottle that you haven't kept an eye on. People slip drugs in them."

"They what?"

"Drugs. So they can rape without the victim remembering it."

My eyes widen. "No."

Nick sighs. "Don't you keep up on current events? Watch the news?"

I think of my dirty movie obsession and flush. "No, not really."

"You have a lot to learn, Mags? Maggie? What

do people call you?"

"My mother and father always call me Magnolia. Just recently, people started calling me Maggie."

"Do you have a preference?" he asks.

"Maggie," I answer quickly.

"Then Maggie you shall be. Look, I know I come across as a jerk, but most of that is just a tough guy act I put on for my job. If you tell anyone that, I'll deny it and spend the rest of my days harassing the hell out of you with every violation I can get you with. Point is, I want to show you the world the right way. People are going to try to take advantage of your naivety, and I don't want that to happen. Would you consider going to dinner and a movie with me Saturday evening? No pressure for you to do anything but enjoy the evening," he assures, holding up his hands.

"Are you asking me on a date?"

"I am."

I smile broadly. "My first date. Okay. I'll go with you. Do I meet you somewhere? How does this work?"

"We're going to do this right. I'm going to pick you up at your door. Be ready for seven o'clock, okay?"

Inside I'm bursting. "Okay. Seven o'clock on Saturday."

An unenthused Honey stands between Nick and me. "Well, if it isn't the dick."

"Nick," he corrects.

"I hear otherwise," she counters.

"Down, girl. I'm off duty tonight. Just enjoying some time with my new friend, Maggie."

"I'm sure there's motive there, and I can just about guess what that is," Honey says confrontationally.

"Yeah, there is. Maggie's a beautiful woman who can very easily be taken advantage of. There are things she doesn't know about protecting herself that she needs to learn. If I can help her with that, and show her a good time while doing it, what's wrong with that?"

"It's the good time you plan to show her that I'm concerned about," Honey snaps.

"Ask Maggie, I told her that things move at her pace, not mine. I might be a dick, but I know how to be chivalrous, too."

Honey looks toward me, and I nod my head to indicate he's telling the truth.

"I'll be keeping an eye on you," she warns.

"Fine by me," Nick says, matching Honey's tone.

"We're going dance. See you in a few, Dick."

"Nick," he yells after Honey, who is dragging me to the dance floor. I glance back and Nick is all smiles.

"Seriously, Mags. Nick?" Honey says, moving her arms to the beat of the music. I really don't know what to do, so I mimic some of the moves I see others doing.

"He's sweet, but he doesn't want others to know it."

"If you say so. Just don't let him pressure you into anything you're not ready for. Promise me."

"I promise. I love that you worry about me."

"It's an emotion I'm not used to feeling. I like not giving a crap better, but damned if you didn't weasel your way into my heart. Now, that's enough mushy stuff."

"Okay," I say with a laugh. "I'll…." I can't finish my sentence because I'm being hurtled across the dance floor. Two rotund and hippy women dancing on either side of me got a little too close, and with one gyration I'm pinballed into the other, who then propels me across the floor. A loud gasp sounds from the crowd, and pain encompasses my ankle.

Honey is beside me first, then Nick. I'm sitting up, but they are both rambling questions at the same time, so I don't know which to look at or whom to answer.

"Back up, please. Everyone. Give her room to breathe. Please, everyone, take a step or two back." A medic bag plops onto the ground next to me, and I look up to see Jace.

"Maggie?" he asks, squatting beside me. "What happened? Are you okay?"

"Yeah. I was accidentally knocked down, but I'm fine. My ankle hurts a little bit. What are you doing here? I thought you worked for the ambulance service."

"I do," he says, unzipping his bag. "I work here, too."

"Hey, look, Ricky Rescue. I saw the whole thing, and I think she's good. You good, Maggie?"

I look to Nick. "Yeah, I'm okay. My ankle doesn't hurt too badly."

"I don't tell you how to do your job, so maybe you should back off and let me do mine, Nick."

"Look, no disrespect, but I think I'm capable of taking care of my girlfriend."

Jace gives me an inquisitive look. "Girlfriend?" he asks.

"I agreed to a date…"

"It's really none of my business," Jace says hastily. "Would you like me to check out your ankle, or do you think your boyfriend can handle it?"

"Jace, I…" My heart hurts, but I'm not sure why. Jace's mood is off, and I can sense his pain. It has nothing to do with me or Nick; it's something deeper. Maybe he was having lady problems? Regardless, I tell him that I'm fine.

He zips his bag. "Have them page me if you change your mind."

I nod, and he's off. Nick gently helps me from the floor, and I keep my arm tightly around his waist as I hobble off of the floor. He helps me onto a barstool then leans across the bar and has a short conversation with the bartender. I spy Honey walking across the room to speak with a different gentleman. She seems more relaxed than before, so I finally start to relax somewhat. A plastic baggy filled with ice wrapped in a bar towel is passed over to Nick. He sits across from me, turning our stools so we face each other. He lifts my leg so my foot rests between his legs, and then he carefully holds the icepack over the tender spot for me.

"You really don't have to do this," I assure Nick.

"I know I don't have to. I want to, but it's very loud in here. Let me take you to the restaurant. Dessert's on me."

"I don't think…"

"Ah, come on. I'll let your friend know where you'll be, and don't tell me you don't like dessert. Everyone likes dessert. I'll get you a huge chunk of chocolate cake? A wedge of cheesecake? Apple pie? Ice cream? Come on, throw me a bone here," he says with a chuckle.

"Key lime pie is my favorite," I answer.

"I don't know if they have it. Hold on, I'll be right back." He gently moves my foot so he can get off of the stool then replaces it just as softly. He meets up with Honey, and after a conversation that lasts a couple of minutes, he returns. "Your fairy godmother gave me permission to take you for a proper slice of pie. It isn't gonna come from here, so we're off on a little adventure, okay?"

"But, Honey? And how am I going to get home? And what about…"

"Shhh. You're going to be with me, and it's my job to worry about all of that stuff. Your job is to enjoy yourself. *Capisce*?"

My response is a smile. He helps me from the

stool, and for the first time since the incident, I put weight on my ankle. It's not horrendously painful, but it's enough for me to wince.

"Wrap your arms right there," Nick says, pointing to his neck. I do, and he swings me so he's half carrying me on his back, half on his side as he walks through the doors. People give us strange looks while we break through the crowd on the main casino floor, but Nick is quick to joke around. "Don't go into the bar. I don't know who she is, but she won't let go." He comes up with a quick witted comment for each strange look we get, and I'm laughing so hard that I'm almost crying when we reach the exit. Jace gives me a half-hearted salute as we walk through the doors. I give a quick wave back.

"So, this is me," Nick says, setting me down beside a midnight black Challenger. My immediate thought is that the car fits his personality. He starts out of the parking lot, but we're met with a mess of a traffic jam. Standstill traffic for as far as the eye can see. He puts the car into park and turns to look at me.

"Well, this isn't cool. Looks like we're stuck here for a while. Why don't you tell me about yourself?"

"You already know nearly everything about me. Before I met you that night, my life consisted of riding my scooter to the archives building for work. Riding my scooter home from work. In between that, I watched movies and occasionally ate pizza. That's it."

"Your father's a high priced attorney. It seems to me like he'd have the means to make your life a little more enjoyable than that."

"They took me with them on one of their trips. I was left behind, so I quit going after that."

"Why didn't you just do things on your own then?"

I sit in silence while I try to put it into words. "The more invisible I was, the easier my life became."

"But…"

"But what?" I ask.

"But something had to happen to get you to this point, or else you'd still be sitting at home watching your movies. What was it?"

"You sure are inquisitive."

"It's my job."

I nod. "There finally came a point where I didn't want to be invisible anymore. I hatched a stupid plan to get attention, and luckily, it didn't work."

"What was the plan?"

"I can't tell you."

"Why not?" he asks.

"Because…"

"Was it illegal?"

"Yes, but it never worked out, so technically, I did nothing wrong."

His eyebrows arch upwards. "I hope you know that you're going to have to tell me about this maniacal plan of yours."

"Oh, no I don't," I say with a smile.

"Yes, you do," he counters.

"I don't think so."

He touches my cheek with his finger. "Why would someone so special spend her life trying to be invisible?"

"You don't know me well enough to call me special," I say, moving away from him.

"I've been a cop for seventeen years now, and never once have I had a victim, detainee, or anyone else for that matter, catch my attention like you have. There's something very special about you, and that's coming from an asshole like me. Imagine what a goodie-goodie would think."

"You're not an asshole. You just like people to think you're one."

"I guess we both have our secrets, don't we. Now what was your plan?"

"It was so incredibly stupid, and it went nowhere. I could never go through with anything so heinous…"

"Jesus, what in the hell were you considering?"

"For about thirty seconds, I contemplated becoming a serial killer."

The darkened interior of the car filled with laughter. "How'd that work out for you?"

"Not so good once I realized I'm incapable of killing anything."

"Well, for the sake of mankind, I'm glad you're incapable. How far did you get into this scheme of yours?"

"Not very far. I accidentally nicked someone

with a hobby knife at the art store and passed out when I saw the blood. That's how I got my new face. I smashed into the counter then the tile floor. Jace picked me up. Anyway, that's when I knew for sure that my plan was a bust."

"Oh, my God. I can't believe I'm hearing this. This is priceless. Please tell me there's more."

"I accidentally caught myself on fire, and that's why my hair is so short now. Jace was there for that one, too."

"You're making this up."

"How I wish I were," I confide.

"Your secret's safe with me. Promise. How did Honey LeReaux come into the picture?"

"I was looking for a prostitute because I wanted to pay someone to teach me about intimate things. I spooked her, she popped me with a stun gun, and then she felt sorry for me afterwards. I've seen her every day since."

"Wow. This is incredible. I look at you now, and I saw the picture of you then. It's so hard to believe the change. If I saw you walking down the street, I'd think to myself, 'There goes a confident, sexy as hell woman.' Then I'd try to get your number, even though I'd assume you were out of my league."

"Me!? Out of your league? Now that's funny!"

"I'm serious. You're kind hearted, witty, gorgeous as hell…" His gaze settles on me, and the air in the car suddenly changes from lighthearted and carefree to thick and sexually charged. "You said you've been kissed before. Did you like it?"

"Yes," I breathe.

"I really want to kiss you right now," he says swallowing hard. With a boldness I didn't think I possessed, I lean toward him. He meets me halfway, and before I know it, his soft lips are upon mine. Jace's kiss was nice, but Nick—Nick's kiss makes me want to strip naked and let him have his way with me. I'm breathless by the time he pulls away. Gazing deeply into my eyes, he uses his thumb to lightly stroke my lower lip. "I think you've done that more than once."

Still unable to put thoughts into words, I shake my head. He has a glint in his eye as he smirks at me. "Traffic is moving. Put on your seatbelt. I'm taking you to get the biggest slice of key lime pie I can find, and I don't care if we have to travel to Florida to find it."

Nick stops at three different all-night diners before he finds one that serves key lime pie. I told him that all the running around was unnecessary, but he insisted. He reclines back in the booth, sipping on his cup of coffee while watching me eat.

"This is so good. You should get yourself a piece." I try to taunt him by slowly pulling the fork out of my mouth after taking a bite. "So good."

"I've never had it before, but I'll buy the entire pie for you if you keep eating it like that."

"You've never tried key lime pie?" I marvel. "And here I thought I was the sheltered one. Here, try some." I put a good sized bite onto the fork and hold it out to him. He looks hesitant at first, but eventually concedes.

"Where have you been all my life?" he asks as his eyes roll up in his head. "That's outrageously good."

I beam. "Told you." I offer him another taste, but he declines. Instead, he waves the server over and requests two more slices. "What's your favorite dessert?" I quiz.

"Nonna's cannoli," he says without hesitation.

"What's cannoli?" I ask.

He gives me a blank stare. "Seriously? You've never heard of cannoli? Oh, you're breaking my heart. I'm making a second date with you even though we still haven't technically had our first date yet. Saturday, we're going to dinner and a movie, but Sunday, you're coming to my Nonna's for Sunday dinner."

"No. No way. I couldn't. Without a doubt, I'll do something to embarrass you, and I'm not going to do that in front of your family."

"*You* aren't the one who has to worry about being embarrassed. *I*, on the other hand, do."

"I'm confused," I confess.

"You won't be after Sunday. Dinner is served at noon. Not a minute before; not a minute after. I'll pick you up at eleven fifteen."

"Nick, this is all moving so fast…"

He covers my hand with his. "Hey, it's just us hanging out and having fun. I won't even kiss you anymore if that will make you feel more comfortable."

"No, don't stop that. You have permission to kiss me anytime you want."

Nick eyes darken. "Do I?"

Looking down at the pie the server deposits on the table, I casually run my fork across the top of it to leave a wavy path of tine marks. "Yes, you do."

He stands, pulls a wad of bills from his pocket, and deposits a couple onto the table. "Let's get out of here."

I'm not sure where he's taking me until I start to realize what part of town we're headed towards. He's taking me to Honey's. Part of me is sad. Part of me is fine with it because I'm getting tired. My ankle was better, but now it's starting to throb some. A few pain relievers, a hot soak in the tub, and a warm bed beckon me. Nick walks me to the door, and before I can finish telling him goodnight, he pulls me close and draws me in for a kiss that lasts at least five minutes. I can barely get the door open before he reminds me about Saturday evening. I nod. "See you Saturday," I promise before closing the door.

"What the fuck?" Honey practically yells as soon as I click the latch into place.

"Why are you yelling at me? I didn't do anything! He was a perfect gentleman all night."

"It's an act."

"It's not. He's sweet. He just can't let people know it because of his line of work. He invited me to dinner and a movie on Saturday and to dinner at his nonna's on Sunday. What's a nonna? Is that his mom? Grandma? Aunt?"

"It's Italian for grandma. He invited you to meet his family?" she asks suspiciously.

"Yes, he did."

Honey relaxes somewhat. "You must've made some kind of impression for him to bring you to meet his family. That's usually a pretty serious step in a relationship."

"Really? Maybe I shouldn't go."

"Go. If anything, you'll get a good meal. The Italians can cook the shit out of anything. Maybe I'm being too harsh on him. My only dealings with him have been law related, and let's face it, we're on different sides of the fence with that one."

"Thanks for agreeing to give him a chance. He really is very sweet. I'm excited for Saturday! What am I supposed to wear? He said he's going to pick me up from here. Should I get him something? Do I offer to pay since he's driving? Help me, Honey!"

"Calm yourself, child! He pays, you don't get him anything, picking you up at the door is the least he can do, and we'll find you something to wear tomorrow. Now, it's bed time for me."

"Okay, Honey. Thank you for tonight."

"I didn't do nothin'. See ya in the morning."

I hobble to the bathroom for a nice long soak. Afterward as I lie on the sofa, I replay the night over and over in my head. I feel myself falling for Nick, but I'm not sure if it's normal. This morning I despised him, then I semi-liked him, and now I'm his girlfriend. His words! Girlfriend. I imagine introducing him to my parents, *Big Daddy and Sunny, I'd liker you to meet my boyfriend, Sergeant Nick Ferrera. I believe you might remember him from some of your court cases, Big Daddy.* I imagine Sunny embracing him, while Big Daddy gives a solid nod of approval. Nick won't be able to take his eyes off me, and I won't take my hands off him. I give a contented sigh. My dreams are going to be some good tonight!

 thirteen

I see that Jace is by himself sitting on the bumper of the ambulance when I bring Honey to the hospital clinic for her follow up. I touch her arm, and she nods, shooing me with her hands. "Go tell him hi. I'm fine. I'll be out as soon as I can."

I follow her advice, and even though I'm practically in front of him, Jace doesn't sense my presence. He looks like shit: blood shot eyes, mussed hair, five o'clock shadow that's working its way towards eight o'clock shadow. "Jace," I call gently.

He snaps out of it. "Oh hey, Mags. How's the ankle?"

"It's fine," I reply, taking a seat beside him. "You okay?"

"Huh? Oh, yeah. I'm good."

"Okay."

"So you're seeing Nick? How's that working

out?"

"I can't really say. We haven't even been on a date yet. We only ran into each other at the club. We started talking, and we hit it off."

"He goes from arresting you to dating you in less than a month. Interesting," Jace comments.

"Am I missing something?" I ask.

"Like what?"

"Like why are you upset about this?"

"Am I?" he remarks.

"Sure seems that way to me. Did I do something wrong?" I draw my hands to my mouth. "Jace, that day you kissed me in the park, was that more than just a pity kiss? Did you…"

"Stop right there. First of all, it wasn't a pity kiss. It was something I wanted to do for you. Second, Mags, I mean this in the nicest way possible, but we can't be more than friends. I'm bad news, and you deserve way better than I could ever give you."

"What do you mean you're bad news? You're the kindest man I know."

"It has nothing to do with kindness, Mags. I work non-stop, and on the rare occasion when I'm not, I'm in a barroom or some place equally depressing. I can't keep a girlfriend because despite their assurances that they're okay with my busy lifestyle, they never really are. Seriously, I enjoy seeing you here and there. I think you're beautiful inside and out, and that any man who lands you is the luckiest guy there is, but that guy can never be me.

Do you understand?"

"I-I think so," I stammer. "I guess I should find Honey. Take care of yourself, Jace."

"Thanks, Mags. You, too."

It's not something I'd normally do, but I feel compelled to kiss his forehead. When I do, he encircles his arms around my waist and hugs me tightly. I hold him back. After a minute or so, he pulls away. "I needed that. Thank you."

I give Jace a smile before strolling off to find Honey. He's gone by the time we leave.

****

Saturday afternoon turns out to be a Honey and Magnolia primp party. A couple of glasses of wine, no serious make up related injuries, and some pulse pounding music make the afternoon fly by. I'm still staring at my reflection when Nick knocks at the door.

I'm wearing black slacks with a sleeveless cowl neck shirt and the same wavy, dark brown wig from before. Plus, Honey outdid herself on my makeup. The only jewelry I'm wearing is a pair of hoop earrings. One look at Nick's face and I know my assessment is right. I'm looking okay.

"Where are ya off to, kids?" Honey asks in a parental fashion.

"Dinner at Chez Fontaine then a movie. It's up to Maggie as to which movie we'll be seeing."

"Oh, I don't know if you should be leaving that

up to me. I don't know much about new releases," I nervously reply.

Nick smiles. "We'll figure it out. Relax. You look beautiful, by the way. I brought these for you," he says, pulling a bouquet of stargazer lilies from behind his back.

"They're beautiful! Oh, Nick. No one has ever given me flowers before. I love them."

Honey takes the bouquet from me. "I'll put them in water. You two get out of here and have a good time. If there's a sock on the door, it means I'm entertaining. Disappear for thirty minutes, then come back."

Nick shoots Honey a warning gaze.

"It's a fucking joke, tight ass. Lighten up."

"Baby steps, Honey. We're not quite there, yet."

"Well, excuse the hell out of me," she snaps.

"Gotcha! See, I'm not the only one who needs loosening up," Nick teases.

"Later, pig."

"In a while, ho."

"Are you two finished?" I ask.

"For now," Honey replies. "You treat my girl right, Nick. You make her cry; I make you cry."

"Understood," he says, holding the front door open for me. He's still chuckling when he gets outside. "That one doesn't hold her tongue at all, does she?"

"No, not usually."

The ride to Chez Fontaine is pretty quiet. Once

we are seated, and our orders have been placed, I decide it's time for Nick to open up to me a little. "You know all about me. Tell me some things about you," I prompt.

"I'm the youngest of six kids, and the only boy, so I had to grow up tough. I guess it's obvious that my family's Italian. Nonna's still old school, but the rest of us are a little more relaxed. My real name is Niccolo; you'll hear that tomorrow. I started working for the PD when I was twenty, and I have been there ever since. Never been married. No kids. Work dominates most of my time, but once I settle down, I plan to correct that. I shoot guns for fun, and I kick ass at poker."

"Are your parents still around?" I ask.

"Yep. Dad's a butcher; Mom's a retired teacher. Angela, Lina, Sofia, Giana, and Rosalie—all teachers."

"Wow. I'm an only child. I can't imagine growing up with that many siblings."

"I got picked on a lot. Dressed up like a baby doll a lot, and if that gets out, you're toast. It really wasn't that fun. It still isn't. They still act like a bunch of mother hens. Again, you'll see tomorrow."

The rest of the night is primarily small talk. The movie is so awful that we leave halfway through and decide to walk along the river front. Nick tells me about some of the most memorable calls he's responded to in regards to the Mississippi River, and I listen in complete fascination. How he was able to keep his cool during some of the situations he describes is beside me. Hearing those stories makes me admire him all the more.

We stop talking for a while, both staring across the river as we watch a huge vessel navigate the channel. It is then, as the wind gently tosses my hair in the breeze that he finally leans in for a kiss. "I should get you home. I don't need Honey to come tracking me down," he teases.

He holds my hand the entire ride to Honey's and gives me another kiss after walking me to the door. Every second I spend with him, I fall harder and harder. Aside from the day we first met, everything he's done or said has been charming. Maybe this is what all the pain and heartache I've felt my entire life has led to? Maybe I'm getting close to my happily ever after? That's the last conscious thought I have before drifting off to sleep.

Honey says I should be a little more casual for Sunday dinner, so I'm dressed in a pair of white capris and an emerald green and white striped, loose fitting blouse. Nick shows up right on time, and he and Honey share a few lines of witty banter before I'm able to get him out the door.

I'm a nervous wreck the entire ride to Nonna's. I'm not good around crowds, I've never been required to meet someone else's family, and as if I'm not socially awkward enough, I'm not up to date on any current events. What am I supposed to talk about with them? Nick stops my nervous hand wringing by covering my hands with his big hand. "Stop. They're going to love you."

Nick pulls his car behind the last of the four in the driveway. We're not even to the back door when I hear loud chatter from inside, and I'm terrified that something is wrong. Nick doesn't even give it a second thought. "Niccolo!" a chorus of female voices calls from inside as soon as Nick crosses the threshold. "Oh, and he's brought a guest to dinner. Quick, Angela, set another place next to Nick for…"

"Maggie. Everyone, this is Maggie," Nick announces to the curious group.

I'm immediately encircled by a gaggle of women all commenting on my hair, my clothes, and my figure. I think some of them introduce themselves, but I can't be sure over the cacophony. They all hug me after completing their inspection, and one by one, they welcome me to the home.

"They tell me that Niccolo has brought a woman to dinner," a matronly woman with silver hair wound into a tight bun says. Her skin is olive and wrinkled, and she wears a simple black dress, rolled stockings, and orthopedic shoes that click when she walks. The room falls silent, and I realize that she's coming towards me.

"Nonna, this is Maggie. Maggie, this is my nonna, Maria Ferrera," Nick says.

"It's very nice to meet you, Mrs. Ferrera," I mumble.

"Does this one eat?" she asks, spinning me

around to give me a once over. "You need fattening up. Come Maggie, you sit; we eat," she says, leading me to the long table laden with dinnerware. "*A tavola*!" one of Nick's sisters yells, and the room suddenly fills with hungry relatives, ages ranging from newborn to elderly.

They must have assigned seating because they automatically veer off in different directions before settling into their seats. Nick pulls out the chair next to him, and once I'm seated, he reaches under the table to give my hand a squeeze. I watch in amazement as noodles are heaped on my plate, a hunk of garlic bread is plopped in front of me, and a pungent cheese is sprinkled over the meatballs and sauce that are now covering the noodle pile.

No one touches his or her fork until Nonna picks up hers and digs in. The room remains silent except for the clinking of silverware against the plates and the occasional cough. I do my best to do what the others are doing, but even though it's probably one of the most delicious meals I've ever had, I have hard time shoveling it down as quickly as they do.

The forks go down, and then the talking starts. Loud talking! Lots of laughter, too. Many of the jokes go over my head, but I still smile and laugh with the rest of the crowd. One of Nick's sisters leans towards me and whispers, "Don't worry. The more time you spend here, the more normal this will become." I smile my thanks to her.

Nonna leaves the table and returns with a massive

tray of cannoli. "For my Niccolo. He loves his Nonna's cannoli." She smacks the hand of the grandson-in-law who tries to take one from the tray. Once Nick grabs one for himself and me, the rest of the tray is emptied by the gang. One bite and I know why Nick loves them so much. The cannoli makes the entire awkward dinner worthwhile.

We leave Nonna's not long after dessert, and Nick gives me a curious look while stopped at a red light. "What?" I ask.

"I was wondering if you'd like to see my place."

He must have seen the uncertainty in my eyes. I'm still not ready for sex! I need to go over a few things with Honey before I take that plunge. "Hey," he says, touching my hand. "No pressure. Just a visit." Nodding, I give him an appreciative smile.

His apartment is small but well furnished. The walls are a dark gray color, the furniture black leather, and though we're in South Louisiana, a fireplace is the focal point of the room.   Mounted above the mantel is the largest television I've ever seen, so large that it practically takes up the entire wall. To the right is a nice, though compact, kitchen with top of the line appliances. A granite topped snack bar separates the kitchen area from the living room. Just beyond the kitchen is a small dining room with a cherry wood table and four chairs. To the left is the bedroom, but the door is cracked so I don't see much of it. Nick notices me checking it out, so he takes my hand in his. "It's okay. Come see."

The door opens, and I'm in love. Room darkening blinds, as well as the dark colors adorning the walls, keep it nice and cozy. The bed is monstrous in size, with a huge, dark wood head and foot board. Across from the bed is a wall of closets. We pass through another doorway, and inside is a bathroom any girl could love. A huge whirlpool tub with three rows of tiled steps sits in the middle of the room. To the right side is a tiled glass-enclosed shower. To the left are his and her vanities, and across the room is another door, which I assume houses the commode.

"I would be happy to live in your bathroom. Seriously, a sleeping bag in the tub, and I'm good."

Nick laughs heartily. "Come check out the bed. Look, no funny business. I keep my promises. See?" He stuffs his hands into his pockets. "Go on. Hop in there and give it a spin."

Curious to see if the bed is as inviting as it looks, I kick off my shoes and climb in; I instantly feel as though I'm wrapped in a warm fuzzy cloud. "Oh, this bed is amazing!" I sing, fighting the urge to crawl under the covers and take a nap.

As if he can read my mind, Nick offers, "Feel free to take a nap if you like. I know I usually do after Nonna's noodles. I think she laces the sauce with sleeping pills." He notices my hesitation. "You can get under the covers, and I'll stay on top if that will make you feel better."

He kicks off his shoes, empties his pockets on top of his dresser, and then takes off his belt and hangs it on a hook inside the closet. He clicks off the light and joins me in the bed. I turn to my side, facing away from him, and he edges closer to spoon with me.

"I thought you said that you were going to stay above the covers," I chide.

"Is this so bad?" he asks, taking my hand in his so he can gently kiss my palm.

"No, not bad at all," I answer with a smile. He laces his fingers through mine and pulls me closer. It's not long before his breathing becomes slow and steady. Mine matches his, and before I know it, I'm asleep, too.

I wake up first, so I take the opportunity to look Nick over. He's incredibly good looking—handsome, rugged, fit. His dark black hair that has a slight wave to it, tanned olive colored skin, and his piercing, brown eyes, even though I can't see them, leave me weak in the knees. I wonder what he looks like naked.

I notice that he's beginning to stir, and I feel like surprising him. He's on his back, so I slide as close to him as possible and roll myself so that half of my body is on top of him. His thick thigh wedges between my legs, and I'm suddenly feeling quite warm.

Without opening his eyes, he slides me higher so that our lips touch. Somewhere during that time, he rolls on top of me, pinning my arms above my head. I'm scared yet aroused at the same time. "Oh, Maggie. You're so beautiful," he breathes into my ear. I wriggle and writhe beneath him, not to get away, but from the pure carnal bliss I'm experiencing. He nuzzles my neck, and I feel it in my core.

"Do you feel me, Maggie? Do you feel what you do to me?" he asks, pressing his solid erection against my thigh.

"You're so big, and hard," I sputter with astonishment.

"You know exactly what a man wants to hear." He kisses me again, this time hard and fervently.

"I do?" I gasp after the kiss.

"Yeah, you do. Can I touch you? Is that okay?" he asks in between short kisses. I nod. He sighs loudly as he takes my breasts in his hands. "Perfect," he mumbles. After a few minutes of kissing and fondling, his hand slowly slides under my shirt, and now he's caressing my breasts through my bra. "Do you want to feel me, Maggie? You can touch it if you want to."

Do I dare? We're already moving faster than the schedule I'd set in my mind. Okay, I have to figure out how far I'm willing to go, and I have to do it quickly. Do I want to touch his penis? Yes. Am I ready for him to see me naked? Not really, but what he's doing to my breasts makes me wonder what he'd do to them if they were bare. I remember Honey telling me about all the things guys like to do with boobs. Decision time: I won't have sex, but maybe I could try some of the things he's willing to teach me.

Up first, feeling a penis for the first time ever!

The thought makes me want to giggle out loud, but I don't dare. A grin spreads across my face as my hand slowly inches towards his erection. He sucks in a breath when I touch him over his pants. "Ah, Maggie," he breathes. His hand beside mine, he fumbles for his zipper.

Oh, my gosh! I'm not only going to touch it; I'm about to see it! A real one. Not a plastic one, not one on TV, an in-the-flesh honest-to-goodness dick. I choke back the nervous laughter that threatens to escape. He slowly drops his pants, and his erection springs forward like a mighty beast. I'm curious, impressed, and uncertain all at the same time. What do I do? Think! What did the women in the pornos do? Part of me wants to swat it around like a cat toy, but I'm pretty sure that's not right. Then it all comes flooding back to me. Hambo the military guy told Sally Sweet that tough men like it rough. Nick's a tough guy. A cop is kinda like a military guy, right? I do my best to mimic what she did in the video.

Leaning into him, I kiss him a couple of times before I get the courage to do my special move. He's nice and relaxed, enjoying the attention when I grip his shaft and squeeze it as hard as I can. Nick launches from the bed. "What the fuck?" he screams, just as he trips over the pants pooled around his ankles. He falls forward and a sound comes from him that no human should ever make.

"Nick!" I scream. "What happened? Are you okay?" I squat next to him. He's barely breathing.

It's a struggle, but I finally roll him over to find that his breathing is still insanely ragged, and even though he tries, he's unable to speak. "Nick, I don't know what to do," I cry.

Between shaky breaths, Nick requests, "My penis. Tell me what it looks like."

"Uh, it's straight from the base to about halfway then it kind of points towards your head."

"Oh, fuck," Nick says before losing consciousness. I immediately call for an ambulance, and then toss a sheet over him while waiting for it to arrive. One guess who the responding medic is. I meet him at the door.

"Magnolia, does trouble follow you, or do you make the trouble?" Jace asks as he comes in the door. "What happened this time?"

"First, it's not what you think. Nothing happened."

Jace scrunches his eyebrows, "Okay, whatever. What's the emergency?"

"It's Nick, and it's bad. Quick, in here," I say, leading him and his partner into the bedroom. Nick is just beginning to stir when Jace pulls back the sheet to assess the damage.

He looks as though he wants to puke, and slowly lowers the sheet back into place. "Penile fracture," he says to his partner.

"Pain. Unbearable," a red-faced Nick mutters.

"Gotcha covered," Jace says, pulling a prefilled syringe from his medic bag. After starting an IV, he injects the contents into a port. Within seconds, relief begins to show on Nick's face. "You coming with us to the hospital?" Jace asks, picking up the wrappers left behind.

"Yes. I'm coming," I say, quickly grabbing my purse. I also take Nick's wallet and keys, and after locking up, I dash to catch up with them. Jace's partner jumps in the back with Nick, and once again, I'm sitting up front with Jace.

"Wanna tell me what happened?" he asks.

"Not particularly because it's incredibly embarrassing. But, I'm going to tell you anyway, so you can tell me what I did wrong."

Jace scrunches his nose while scratching the back of his neck. "Lay it on me."

"We were kissing and stuff, and Nick asked me if I wanted to see, you know, *it*. He unzipped his pants, *it* popped out, but I didn't know what to do with, you know, *it*. Then I remembered a movie I watched where Hambo tells Sally Sweet that tough guys like it rough. She was gripping and massaging *it*, and he kept asking her to do it harder. I figure that since Nick is a cop, that he might like it that way, so I gave it a squeeze."

"Jesus, Mags! How hard did you squeeze it to make it snap like that?" Jace questions.

"I didn't do that! That happened when he launched out of bed, and the pants he was wearing got caught around his ankles. He tripped and fell. That's how it got crooked."

"I can't believe I'm asking this. Mags, when you were doing the whole touching thing, did you start out slowly and work your way to something a little rougher, or did you just go for it?"

"I just went for it."

Jace winces. "That's what went wrong. If you learn anything from this, know that penises are pretty sensitive. You don't have to be rough with them. Start soft, and if the man you're with wants it rougher, he'll let you know. Okay?"

I nod, tears starting to well in my eyes. "How bad did I hurt him?"

"He's going to be out of commission for a while, and it'll be a painful recovery."

"Do you think I should leave? I'm sure he hates me."

"Only one way for you to find out, Mags, and that involves sticking around."

"I guess you're right. At the very least, I owe him an apology."

"I think that's a good call," Jace affirms.

They wheel Nick into the ER, but I'm not allowed past admitting. I give as much information as possible to the admin clerk before taking a seat. A few hours later, a nurse comes for me.

"Excuse me, are you with Nick Ferrera?"

"I am," I answer, tossing aside the magazine I'm thumbing through.

"He's asking for you. You can follow me."

I do as she requests, but suddenly freeze when I

arrive at Nick's cubicle. The nurse gives me a reassuring smile and a pat on the shoulder before bustling off to do some paperwork. I slowly pull the curtain back to find Nick semi-reclined in the bed. His eyes are closed, but when he hears the curtains rustling, he opens them.

"Maggie?" he asks.

I move a little closer. "Yeah, it's me. Nick, I'm so sorry.."

"Shhhh," he says, sloppily bringing his fingers to his lips. "Don't blame yourself for this. It's my fault. I should have talked you through it a little more. I sometimes forget that you... Well, anyway. Please don't do that again. That was bad. Before was good, but that was bad, bad, bad. No squeezy, wheezy." He giggles. "No grip, trip." He giggles again. "No clench, flinch."

"I promise. Are you in pain?"

"Not anymore," he says with a sloppy grin.

"Should I call someone from your family to sit with you?"

"Nope. They're letting me go home, but I'll need someone to stay with me. You up for it? I promise, no funny business." He laughs hysterically. "Wait. I forgot. You broke my penis."

"Nick, I feel terrible." He reaches out to cover my mouth.

"Shhhh. No apologies. My pee-pee is broken, but I can still kiss those luscious lips of yours. Come here, sweetheart," he says, pulling me towards him.

"Nick, I don't think…" He kisses me long and hard, but mid-kiss he pulls away.

"Nope. Can't kiss you like that. More swelling going on. Not good." He pulls the covers back to reposition an ice pack that is placed over the area. "Ah, better. Remember when I held your ice pack after you hurt your ankle? Will you hold mine?" he asks, laughing. The laughing stops almost immediately, "Owww, no thinking that way either. Swelling." He takes a deep breath and then spews a number to me. "Call him. His name is, oh fuck, what is his name? Oh yeah, Porkchop. He's my friend and he will come to get us, and he'll bring us home."

"Porkchop?" I ask to be sure I'd heard correctly.

"Yup. Pooooorkchoooooopah"

I dial the numbers, and a man answers on the second ring. "Hello, Mr. Chop? Porkchop?"

"Who is this?" he asks.

"I'm Maggie Berrybush, and I'm a friend of Nick's. He had an accident, but he's fine. He's being discharged from the hospital and needs a ride home. He said I should call you."

"What in the hell did he do now? Did that dumb ass finally go for a swim in the gator pond?"

"Huh? No. He fell and hurt something."

"Something? What something? His arm, his leg, his wrist?"

"His penis." I heard Porkchop wince through the phone.

"Awww, shit man. That's bad news. Look

Maggie, give me ten minutes, and I'll be there."

Porkchop is true to his word and arrives within ten minutes. He looks every bit as I'd imagined: rotund, long scruffy beard, grease stained shirt, and a badge hanging around his neck.

"So I hear you broke your dick. They tell me they splinted it with a set of toothpicks." Porkchop loudly teases Nick before turning to me. "My apologies for the foul language, but it's too good of an opportunity to let pass by."

I'm not sure if it's his size or his loud and crass nature, but I'm extremely intimidated by this man. "Uhm, it's fine. T-thank you for coming to get us."

"No problem. I had some business in the area anyway. Come on, let's get this sad sack of shit into the car. I'm parked on the ER ramp."

"I hear you," Nick slurs.

"What's your point?" Porkchop teases.

The only delay in leaving is a slight one as the nurse helps to get Nick into a wheelchair. After that, everything sort of falls into place. Porkchop helps me get him inside and into the bed. Nick's out cold, so he's no problem. Porkchop also volunteers to get Nick's scripts filled and to pick up a few things from the grocery store, so I readily take him up on that offer. "Anything else" he asks as he glances over the list.

"Yes. Will you tell me why they call you Porkchop?" I finally work up the nerve to ask.

"It's kind of a vulgar story. I'll try to clean it up

some. Me and my buddy were banging this super rich married woman one night…"

"You know, maybe you should save that story for another time? I think I hear Nick moaning in there; he could probably use those meds."

"Oh, yeah. I'll be right back," he says with a lopsided grin. Once he's gone, I wonder who the buddy is that he was talking about. Surely it wasn't Nick? Maybe it was? Maybe one day I'll get up the nerve to ask Nick about it. For right now though, my focus is on him and his recovery. He barely stirs when I change out the icepack, so I lightly kiss his forehead before settling onto the sofa with a book.

Porkchop comes and goes with the supplies, and I take a minute to call Honey to fill her in on the latest. She vows that we're going to run through the full spectrum of intimacy possibilities once I make it back to her place so there will be no future concerns about such an event occurring again. It's late by the time we disconnect, so I quickly search through Nick's dresser drawers for something to wear. I find a set of pajamas, but the bottoms are way too big to even consider donning, so I carry just the top into the bathroom with me.

I pull off my wig, and run my fingers through my hair. It's looking pretty good, so I decide to ditch the fake hair and go short for a while. Everything in Nick's shower smells like him, but I don't mind so much. I soap up, rinse off, and slip into the pajama shirt. After smoothing my hair back into place, I check on the patient. He's still out, so I very gently slip into bed beside him, but I don't rest until I'm sure there is a channel of pillows protecting his lower half. I definitely don't want to add insult to injury with an accidental kick in the middle of the night.

I awaken to the sound of Nick whimpering. I slowly pull my eyes open to find him looking my way. "Cover it," he says, his hands on his crotch. "Owww. It hurts so bad."

I sit up quickly in the bed. "Cover what? What's happening?"

He looks like he's fanning his chest with his hand. "Your body. All of it. Blood rushing to bad places. Hurts."

"But I'm dressed," I argue.

He shifts around uncomfortably. "I can see the swell of your breast through the fabric, and now, those long creamy white thighs of yours. Oh, fuck!" he snaps his eyes closed. "Ah! I still see it in my mind. Make it go away."

I madly dash to the bathroom to put on what I was wearing the day before. "Is this better?"

He cracks an eye open. "A little," he says, blowing through the pain like a woman in labor. "Maggie, I appreciate that you want to take care of me, but I don't think it's going to work. I'm too attracted to you, and when I think or see certain things... Well, you see what happens. I'll call my mom to come take care of me. It'll make her day for me ask for her help."

"But I feel like I should be the one taking care of you since this is all my fault," I explain.

"No, I bear equal fault in this. I moved things along too quickly."

"Nick, I…"

He holds up his hand. "We can talk about all of this later. How about you give me a call tonight?"

I nod. "I'll call around seven."

"Seven it is," Nick agrees with a grimace.

I'm feeling a little forlorn when I leave his apartment, but I'm also sure that he'll be in good hands. If anyone can get him up and around quickly, surely it's his mother. But what is he going to tell her about the accident? Will she know that I broke her son's pee-pee? How utterly embarrassing! I may never look her in the eye again.

Honey's still sleeping when I get back to her house, but I'm too charged to sit around and wait for her to wake up. I change into a pair of running shorts and a t-shirt then make my way to the park that Jace frequents. He says running clears his mind and relieves his stress. Maybe it's time I give it a try?

I take off at a full run as soon as I hit the path, and I'm a gnarled up, writhing mess by the time I make it to the wooded area. I roll around on the ground, desperate for the muscles in my legs to relax, but it seems like the more I move, the tighter they constrict.

"Ma'am, are you okay?" I recognize his voice instantly. "Magnolia? I should have guessed."

"Jace, help me. Make the pain stop. Cramps!"

He's laughing so hard that he starts to cough. I should be offended, but the pain is too intense.

"Jaaaacccceee! Helllllp!"

"Okay, okay." He kneels on the ground next to me, takes one ankle in his hands, and props it on his shoulder. He interlocks his fingers and slowly begins to press down on my knee. The relief is nearly instantaneous, and I beg him to do the other side, too.

"Just give it a second. Let's make sure this one is stretched out good, first." He manipulates my leg a little more before putting it flat on the ground then he repeats the process with the next one.

"Am I that out of shape?" I ask. "Your legs don't cramp up like this when you're running."

"Did you hydrate and stretch before you started?" he inquires.

"Huh?" I ask.

Jace chuckles as he continues to stretch me. "Oh, Maggie. So much to learn. Speaking of, how's the boyfriend?"

"In pain."

"I bet."

"Thank you for taking care of him."

"Just doing my job."

"Yeah, but still…"

"You're welcome. So, you've decided to become a runner?"

"You said it helps you, so I figured I'd give it a try."

"Well, let me give you a few pointers so you don't end up like this again. The next person to find you contorted up on the ground while writhing in agony might call a priest for an exorcism."

"It wasn't that bad," I fuss.

He lifts his brows. I hang my head. He tucks his finger under my chin. "Hey, I needed that laugh. I'm glad I found you in the throes of agony."

"Happy I could help," I say, sardonically. Jace ignores it.

"I'm starting to sense a theme in our conversations lately, Mags. Let's talk about what went wrong…" He gives me about a ten minute lecture on running: the before, the during, and the after. Apparently, there is a process to follow, and you can't simply take off running. Who knew?

He convinces me to try again, but this time, he guides me in some stretches before we start out. I notice that it not only feels better physically, but the time goes by much quicker when someone is running with me. I'm tired, but overall, I feel good when we stop.

"I kept up with you pretty good, didn't I?" I ask, bending at the waist.

"You did great," Jace praises.

"One lap around the park. Is that good?"

"For your first time, it is."

"How many laps do you do?" I inquire.

"Five when I don't have much time, ten otherwise."

I nearly fall over. Jace laughs.

"I didn't start out that way. You'll build up to it."

"If you say so."

He looks down at his watch. "Anyway, I have to get going. Remember to hydrate and stretch before your next run!" he calls as he jogs down the path. "Take care, Mags."

"Bye, Jace. See you around?"

"Here, fine. Ambulance, no!" he says with a laugh before sprinting off.

fourteen

Three weeks pass, and I've run into Jace a handful of times on the running path. I'm able to keep up with him for three to four laps, but he smokes me after that. Some days he's carefree and in a great mood, some days he's quiet and withdrawn. I repeatedly ask him if he wants to talk about it, but he always declines the offer. Those days, we run in silence, simply taking solace in each others' company.

Nick is well on the mend and feels as though he's ready to see me. We've only talked on the phone since the incident, so I want to look extra special when I see him tonight. He's taking me dancing at one of the local clubs, and I can't wait! Honey has given me a few dance lessons, so I'm ready to show off my new moves.

It's amazing how much my hair has grown out. It's no longer pixie style but in an inverted bob. I'm wearing a silky garnet colored halter top, dark jeans, and strappy sandals with a kitten heel. My lips match my top, my eyes are smudged smoky black, and I'm sans jewelry tonight. I smile at my reflection.

As usual, Nick is right on time, and he's all smiles when he sees me. "Wow, you just took my breath away," he says.

I go up on my tip toes to give him a kiss; then rethinking it, I quickly take a step back. "I don't want to hurt you. I'm sorry."

"Nah, it's all good, baby. Come here," he says, taking me into his arms. "I missed you."

"I missed you, too," I confess. He kisses me in a way that nearly makes up for the weeks we spent apart, and I want him to take me right then and there.

"You ready?" he asks, still holding me in his arms.

I nod because I'm not capable of coherent speech.

The club is packed when we arrive, and Nick has a hard time getting to the bar for our drinks. "Maybe we should rethink this?" he asks, as we fight our way through the crowd.

"Let's have at least one drink and one dance, okay?" I ask.

He touches my face. "Anything you want, princess." Sigh.

We finally get to the bar, and lo and behold, there sits Jace in the arms of three different women. The one on his right is stroking his hair, the one on the left has her head on his shoulder, and the one standing between his legs is playing with the buttons on his shirt.

"Who'd have guessed that driving an ambulance would get someone so much attention?" Nick comments. I stay quiet. I'm not sure why, but that punched-in-the-stomach, heart hurting feeling is back. I try to ignore him, but I can't seem to break my gaze. Jace finally notices me, and he snaps to attention.

"Mags, didn't expect to see you here. Good to see you up and around," he directs towards Nick. "Guess that means Nick's dick is healed. That was quick, but then again, the smaller the package…"

Nick starts to move toward him, but I put my hand on his chest. I feel a low grumbly growl bellowing in his chest. Jace grins broadly and takes a pull from his beer. A slow song is playing, so I plead with Nick to dance with me. He obliges, and I nestle my head on his shoulder as we slowly sway back and forth to the beat of the music.

I open my eyes to see Jace and two of his scantily clad lady friends practically dry humping on the dance floor. One is in front of him riding his leg, while the other is behind him grinding against his body. I'm repulsed by the sight, so I turn my head to rest on Nick's chest. He wraps his arms around me pulling me closer to his body. I feel safe, warm, and content. The song ends much too quickly, and I'm sad to hear a high energy dance track pulse through the room.

I'm shocked and appalled by the obscenities that are spewing out of Jace. "Yeah baby! I'm riding you tonight!" he yells. "And you, and you…" He points to each of the scantily clad women around him, and they take turns squealing with delight.

"Real classy, Jace," Nick scolds.

"I don't remember asking your opinion, Nick," he says confrontationally.

"You got it anyway. Consider it a gift."

"Fuck you and your gift."

"He's drunk. Let's go. I don't want to be here anymore," I say, standing between Nick and Jace.

Nick's jaw is tightly set, and the stare that he's giving Jace intimidates the hell out of me. His face relaxes; he pops his neck from side to side, then looks to me. "Sure. Let's get out of here. There's more privacy at my place anyway, and I'm thinking I want to be alone with you." He kisses me passionately right there in the middle of the dance floor, and I'm still flabbergasted when he takes my hand to lead me out of the club.

Jace's face is red, and his nostrils flared, and for a second, I worry that he's going to go after Nick. Instead, he starts making out with the girl in front of him. I sadly shake my head as Nick pulls me through the crowd. I'm feeling queasy, so I apologize to Nick and ask him to bring me home. He understands, even going so far as stopping at a drug store along the way to buy me some medicine. I promise to call him the next day.

I don't sleep very well that night, so first thing in the morning I hit the running trail. I know that there is no way in hell that I'll be running into Jace this time. Assuredly, he's passed out naked surrounded by a slew of loose women. I'm angry at first. With each step, I gain a little momentum, until I'm finally at a full run. When did Jace become such an asshole? I've never seen him act that way, and I wonder if it only happened because he was drinking. My mind plays out other scenarios, but none of them make sense.

After the first lap, my anger begins to dissipate because I think back to my night with Nick. He's the total package. I broke his penis, yet he still wants to be with me. That says a lot about the man. I'm off basking in my daydream, when I'm suddenly tossed to the ground. A man wearing a hood jumps on top of me, and I'm too stunned to react.

"Money!" he demands, a knife glinting in his hand.

"I-I-I don't have any," I say, holding my hands up to try to protect my neck and face.

"Bullshit! Where is it? Shoe or bra?"

"Neither," I pant because I can't catch my breath.

The knife is poised to slash my shirt, when the hooded assailant is suddenly tossed off me. Jace jumps on top of him and begins beating the ever living crap out of the guy. The thrashing is so brutal that I have to pull Jace away from him. "He's out! Jace! Stop! He's not moving anymore!"

Jace snaps out of it and stares down at the bloodied man while he tries to catch his breath. "You okay?" he asks, standing up.

"I'm fine. Scared, but fine," I answer. I'm shaking far too hard to call anyone, so I'm glad that Jace decides to call the police. As soon as he disconnects from the dispatcher, I begin to cry.

"Don't cry, Mags. Come here," he says, pulling me into his arms. "Are you sure you're okay."

Sniveling into his chest, I manage to give him a nod. It takes me about a minute or so to compose myself, and I pull away to dash the tears from my eyes. "I didn't expect to see you here today," I comment between sniffles.

"Why not?"

"Last night. The club."

"What about it?" he asks.

"Seriously?" I fuss.

"Didn't we discuss this not that long ago? I'm no good for anyone. I work, I drink, I screw, I run—end of story. That's my life. It's not a secret, Mags. You heard it straight from me."

"But Jace, I see something different. I was actually shocked by your behavior because that's not the Jace I know."

"No, sweetheart, *that* is the real Jace you saw. Sorry to disappoint you."

I shake my head while giving him a look of disbelief. As hard as I shake my head, he nods.

"Your boyfriend's here," Jace says, signaling toward the road. Nick, dressed in jeans and a t-shirt, rapidly exits the passenger side of an unmarked police cruiser. He has a badge around his neck and a gun strapped to his thigh, as does the man who gets out of the driver's side. They hastily make their way towards Jace and me, where they look from me to Jace to the battered man on the ground.

"You do this?" Nick asks Jace.

"Yeah."

"You okay?" Nick asks me in a much softer tone.

"Yeah, I'm shaken up, but I'm okay."

"What happened?" Nick inquires.

"I was here for a run, and this guy knocks me to the ground, pulls a knife, and wants money. I told him I didn't have any, and he was about to cut my shirt open, but Jace stopped him."

"I'll say he did. Is he breathing, Jay?"

Jay, the other police officer, leans down to assess the suspect. "Yeah, he's breathing. His face ain't so pretty, but he's okay. Maybe he'll learn his lesson about robbing women at knifepoint?" He clicks the bracelets of a set of handcuffs into place before trying to rouse the man. "Hey. Hey dude. Wake up." He stands and rocks the man with his shoe. He starts to stir a little bit, and when he realizes where he is and what has happened, he tries to jump up to run. He doesn't get far because Jay sticks out his foot to trip him. He stumbles forward, and hits the ground head first. He comes up with a mouthful of grass and leaves, not to mention the dirt that clings to the bloody mess. He doesn't look so hot, and I do my best to fight the urge to faint.

"We gotta get this guy processed," Nick says

pulling me aside. Standing close to me, he lowers the volume of his voice. "Are you sure you're okay? I need to know if he hurt you."

"My knees are kind of wobbly, but I'm fine, I promise. He startled me more than he hurt me. I'm glad Jace showed up when he did." A shudder runs through my body. Nick takes my face in his hands and plants a gentle kiss on my forehead. "You did good, Maggie, but maybe we should talk about you finding another place to run or maybe getting you some self-defense items?"

"Okay," I agree. "We'll talk about it more later. I know you have to go."

"Hey, Rocky," Nick says to Jace. "You think you can bring her home? I'd take her, but we gotta take this trash to the station for booking."

"Yeah. Sure. No problem," Jace agrees.

"Good. Thanks. You come down to the station later to give a statement, okay?" He instructs Jace before he turns to me. "I'll get yours when I see you tonight." I nod, and he gives me a quick kiss on the lips before joining Jay, who is walking the criminal to the unmarked unit.

"Let's go. I have to get to my shift," Jace says, walking towards his truck in the parking lot.

"You're working again today?" I ask.

"What of it?" he asks.

"You might not be as grumpy if you didn't work all of the time."

He rolls his eyes. "Well, by all means, let me

quit picking up extra shifts so I won't be so grumpy."

"What's wrong with you? Why are you acting this way?"

Jace stops the truck and moves so that his face is inches from mine. "For the last time, this is me. It's not an act. There's nothing wrong with me. It's just who I am. I'm sorry if you don't approve, but to be honest, I don't care. I'm happy to be your running companion and to patch you up when you get hurt, but I'm no one's knight in shining armor. You have Nick for that, so how about you lay off the criticism when it comes to my life?"

I set my jaw. "Fine. If that's how you want it."

"It's how it has to be."

"Whatever." I can't get out of the truck fast enough. In fact, I jump out before it comes to a complete stop. I stumble a bit, but don't even look back as I trudge up the drive to Honey's house.

I shower, nap, and then await Nick's arrival once he gets off his shift. It's dark by the time he knocks on the door.

"Hi, sweetness. Can I come in?"

"Of course," I say with a smile.

"We have paperwork to do," he says, holding up a file folder.

"That's fine," I answer, pointing him towards the sofa. My statement doesn't take too long, and once I'm finished, Nick tucks it into the folder and tosses it onto the coffee table. I stretch out, putting my head in his lap, and he kicks his legs onto the coffee table. I close my eyes to better enjoy the feel of him running his fingers through my hair. This feels nice, comfortable, and natural. We're not speaking, not making out, just enjoying being with each other. He clicks the remote until he finds a football game he wants to watch, and I daydream about a future where we're doing this in our house. The more time I spend with him, the more I think that he might eventually become "the one."

After the game, we talk about my running habits, and he runs through some safety suggestions. He wants to teach me how to shoot a gun and to equip me with mace, a stun gun, and a host of other things. I tell him I'll consider each of them and get back to him. He leaves not long after our conversation, but not before a nice, passionate make out session that leaves us both begging for cold showers.

Later that night, I think of all the options he's given me, and I decide that the mace is probably my best bet. I could call him, but instead, I decide to surprise him at the station the next day. There's another surprise for him, too. I've decided that Nick should be my first, and I'm ready to take the plunge. I'm almost giddy thinking of what his reaction will be. I know he's going to be happy about my decision, and I also know that he'll make my first time extra special.

The next morning, I spring out of bed, thoroughly excited about the new day. I take my time putting on my makeup and fixing my hair just right, before sliding on a pair of jeans and a lacy emerald green blouse. I'm happy with my reflection, so I call a cab to take me to town. The driver stomps on the gas as soon as I exit the cab, and I'm left alone on the street in front of the sterile looking building.

There are about ten steps to the front door, so I take them two at a time and practically run into a gentleman who is exiting as I'm entering. "I'm so sorry," I say, thankful I didn't tumble the ten steps down.

"My fault," he says. "I haven't seen you around here before. Is there something you need help with?"

"I'm here to see Nick Ferrera. I'm his girlfriend, Maggie."

"Maggie. I've heard a lot about you. Come with me. I'll bring you to him," he says with a huge smile.

"Nick talks about me?" I ask.

"All the time," the mystery man replies. Hearing that makes me feel great. He uses a passkey to open a few doors, and finally, he leaves me standing in a hall. "Nick's office is the last one on the right once you make that corner at the end of the hall. He should be in there, but if he's not, just wait for him. He's floating around here somewhere."

"Thank you." The man shuts the door as he leaves, and I'm suddenly alone in the corridor. I start in the direction he pointed me, and as soon as I round the corner, I hear loud talking and laughter. The door that the man said is Nick's is cracked open, and the sounds are coming from inside. Not wanting to disturb him since he is obviously with others, I quietly wait at the end of the hall.

"...she has no clue. She's putty in my hands." I recognize the voice as Nick's.

"But dude, she broke your dick," says a voice I don't recognize.

"Yeah, but she's smokin' hot, and she's a virgin. As long as she don't cut the sucker off, I'm fine. Knowing how good it's going to feel to dive into that unchartered territory, I'm getting hard just thinking of it." Laughter spills from the room. "Think about it. I'm getting old, man. The chance of bagging a virgin is practically nil, much less one who looks good. That bitch is my conquest, and you know what? She's gonna squeal with delight when I give it to her."

"Is it true you took her to meet your family? That has to mean something," says another voice I don't recognize.

"It means I'm gonna get Momma and Nonna to cater to my every whim when I tell them I had to break up with her because I caught her cheating on me."

"That's cold, man. I can't believe you're going to play that girl like that. Fuck her, and dump her. That's harsh."

"I do it all of the time. No sweat off of my back. How do you think I got the name Nick the Dick? I earned that bitch." More laughter spills from the room, and I'm going to be sick. I run out the door, down the hall, and into the ladies room where I dry heave until tears flood my eyes. I sink to the floor, and I want to cry, but the only tears that will come are the ones that accompany the heaving.

I want nothing more than to be as far away from the building as possible, so I stumble my way out of the bathroom and, though I get some strange looks along the way, out of the door. I pull out my cell phone and try to call Honey, but it goes directly to her voicemail. There is only one other person I know I can talk to, and though he's an ass, he's a shoulder to cry on.

"Jace?" I sniffle. "Are you at work?"

"No, just getting off a shift. Are you okay, Mags? What's wrong?"

"I'm not okay. Can you come get me?" I ask.

"Where are you?"

"The park near the police station where Nick works."

"I'm on my way."

I end the call and tuck the phone into my purse. I manage to take a few deep breaths before Jace arrives. I think I'm doing well, but as soon as I see him, the tears flow freely. He looks concerned as he walks me to his truck and helps me into the passenger side. Once he's in the cab, he asks, "Do you need a doctor? Are you hurt?"

I shake my head. "Can we go to your place? I want out of here."

He looks hesitant at first, but then he puts the truck into gear and veers into traffic. We reach a very nice stucco apartment complex, and he pulls into a parking spot somewhere in the middle of the well-manicured facility. He opens the door to the first apartment on the left, and then holds his hand out usher me inside.

Though elegant, his apartment is very sparsely furnished and extremely plain. The walls are white, there is a sofa and a TV, but that's all. It's obvious that he doesn't spend very much time at his place.

"Have a seat," he offers. I take him up on the offer, and after plucking a box of tissue from the snack bar, he sits beside me.

"I know you're probably not going to care about this, nor do you really want to hear it, but I need someone to talk to. Honey isn't answering her phone, so she must be with a client." Jace stays quiet, but gives me a look that says he wants further explanation. "I overheard something just now. A private conversation Nick was having with some of his co-workers. Everything has been an elaborate ploy so he can take my virginity then dump me. Jace, the things that came out of his mouth. Things like, 'I'm gonna make that bitch squeal,' and 'I fuck and dump all the time. How do you think I got the name Nick the Dick? I earned that bitch.' He's never been anything but charming around me, and I fell for it. Oh, my God. I fell for it." I begin to sob. "I went to the station to tell him that I was ready. I'm such a fool."

Jace pulls me close, and hugs me tightly. "You're not a fool. You had no way of knowing that he was taking advantage of you."

"Being an ugly freak is so much easier than this shit. How am I ever supposed to trust anyone again? When am I going to know it's for real and not because I'm being used? He took my dignity, Jace. How can I ever look anyone in the face again? There's no telling how many people he's bragged to about his plan. I'm so humiliated."

"I'm sorry, Mags. I know you're hurting now, but please don't judge all men based upon his actions. Not all of them are bad news."

"I don't know, Jace. I'm ready to quit. I think I'm going to talk to Big Daddy to see if I can come home. I think he'll be okay with it."

"And then what? You're going to go back to hiding from the world? Damn it, you were given the gift of rebirth, and you're just going to throw it away?"

"I'm scared. I don't want to live in your world anymore."

"It's your world, too! You just choose to ignore it."

"I'm done," I say, my voice laden with defeat.

"Me, too. I'm not going to beg you to stick around. If you want to give up, then so be it. I'll bring you back to Honey's." He makes a grab for his keys, and storms off to the front door. He angrily taps his foot while holding it open for me. We're both silent on the ride back to Honey's. He's silent when he drops me off, too. I get out of the truck, and he drives away.

Heavy hearted, I begin to pack my things. I don't even have the heart to dig the scooter from Honey's garage, so I call a cab instead. I'm sure Big Daddy can find someone to fetch it for me later.

Once home, I explain to him some of what has happened, and he agrees that I can have my old garage apartment again. The first thing I do is make it look less like the abode of a sex-starved teen and more like an adult woman is in residence.

Sunny is happy to help me pick some new paint colors and furniture, and I actually enjoy spending time shopping with her for these things. A few days after moving back home, Big Daddy finds Sunny and me sitting at the kitchen table discussing a bathroom remodel for me. He tosses his thick leather briefcase onto the counter, then in his usual melodramatic voice, he begins, "I suppose I can finally divulge my recent whereabouts since the issue has now been adjudicated. Would you care to guess the matter of which I'm speaking, Magnolia?"

"No, Big Daddy. I have no idea what you're talking about."

"Ah, well, let me enlighten you." He begins to pace up and down the length of the kitchen, his index fingers on the bridge of his nose. "Two nights ago, I received an urgent phone call from one Jace Taylor, who informs me that he's being detained for assault and battery on one Sergeant Niccolo Ferrera. It seems that Mr. Taylor caused severe personal injury to

Sergeant Ferrera's face, said injury requiring stitches and a jaw realignment for the Sergeant. After meeting with representatives of all sides, Sergeant Ferrera insisted the charges be dropped, and has since been put on administrative leave for provoking the aforementioned attack. No future legal ramifications will come from the incident. Your friend is a very lucky man."

I finally get over my shock enough to ask, "How's Jace?"

"Mr. Taylor is fine. He left the conference and went right back to work."

I sigh with relief.

For the first time ever, Big Daddy struggles to find the right words. "Magnolia, there was full disclosure at the meeting, and I want you to know that you are welcome to stay with us as long as you desire. I'm full of remorse for forcing you to leave before. I suppose I should have thought my plan through a little better. I really thought I'd be helping you."

"It's okay, Big Daddy. I know that your heart was in the right place. Thank you for allowing me to stay."

Sunny looks on curiously, and Big Daddy motions to say that he'll tell her about it later. I ask to be excused, and they both nod. I dash up to my apartment, and once I get to the top, I realize that I haven't done my ritual since moving in with Honey. I'm no longer terrified of stairs. When I get inside, I have a slew of emotions racing through me. Jace beat the hell out of Nick for me. I know without a shadow of a doubt that it was for me, but why? What does it matter to him? He put his job and his life on the line in retaliation of Nick's atrocity. Part of me feels relief that Nick got what was coming to him, but mostly, I feel confused.

I try calling Jace, but he doesn't answer his phone. Tightly hugging my pillow, I curl up in bed and cry until I fall asleep.

I'm standing at the kitchen sink eating a spoon of peanut butter. Three weeks have passed since the Jace/Nick showdown, and I haven't heard from either one of them. Though I've reverted back to being an introvert, I do occasionally get out of the house. Big Daddy has been giving me driving lessons, and I've done so well that there is a somewhat shiny, ten-year-old Toyota in the driveway.

I drive to the store every once in a while to try on some clothes or to buy something pretty for my apartment. Sometimes, I visit with Honey. She says that word on the street is that Nick packed up and left Baton Rouge. He's supposed to have a job in New Orleans or a surrounding area. As long as I don't have to see him, I couldn't care less. Honey has tried on several occasions to set me up on blind dates, but I always decline. I can tell that it makes her upset, but she doesn't harp on it much.

I toss the empty spoon into the sink and walk down the long corridor by Sunny's art studio. It's lesson time, and nothing has changed. Saggy balls and droopy boobies are everywhere. I even spy Diablo in the corner. A shudder runs through my body. I don't realize that I'm staring, but some of the old men do. My thoughts are on Jace and the day he came to the house to pick up the patients. Then I think about how he came back and took care of me after the pig leg incident. He can't be all bad, despite his insistence on the contrary.

The room comes back into focus, and I notice two of the old men making googly eyes at me. Sunny notices me standing at the window and shrugs as if to say, "Is everything okay?" I nod and move away from the classroom. I hear one of the old men ask when I'll be joining the class. Pervs!

I go upstairs and put on a pair of running shorts, shoes, and a tank top. It's been so long since I've felt a real honest-to-goodness endorphin release, so I grab my keys and head to the trail.

I take my time stretching, and also use the time to scan the area for any unwanted guests. The park appears to be deserted, so once I'm limbered up, I start down the asphalt path. I let my mind wander, and I think of how far I've come in a relatively short time. My heart is beginning to heal from the hurt caused by Nick, and though I'm not ready to throw myself out there, I realize that I'm not completely opposed to the idea of dating again. I also realize that being the way I was before the transformation is incredibly boring. I vow to find some hobbies, and I'm not talking about nude art lessons. I'm thinking that learning a martial art wouldn't be a bad thing. Maybe I could learn to play tennis or golf? I'd keep an eye out for something that interests me. Hell, maybe I'll even go back to school.

I'm pondering degree programs when I stumble across something on the path and land head first into a pile of leaves. Shaking them off me, I blow pine needles from my lips. "Yuck!" I'm pretty sure I tripped over a log, so my intention is to move it off the path before someone else trips over it. My heart sinks when I notice Jace sprawled out on the ground. His back is propped up against a tree, and his feet are extended out in front of him. I had tripped over his legs.

"Jace!" I cry, tapping his cheek. "Jace! Wake up!"

He barely stirs, but my heart starts to beat again when I realize he's alive. "Jace! Please! Look at me." I scan his body and notice that his knuckles are bloodied, bruised, and swollen. A bottle of whiskey is to his right and a baseball cap to his left. He's not in his running attire; instead, he wears a simple gray jogging suit.

I give him a hearty shake, and he struggles to open his eyes. "Mags? Is that you?" His breath practically knocks me on my ass.

"Yeah, it's me. Had much to drink, Jace?" I ask, taking a seat next to him.

"Why yes, I did."

"Want to tell me what happened?" I ask, taking his hand in mine so I can get a better look at his injuries. He pulls it away from me.

"I'm fine."

"No, you're not. You look like shit. What happened?"

"Nothing for you to worry about. Just finish your run and head home. I'll be fine," Jace insists.

"No way am I leaving you here. Come on. Stand up," I say, wrapping his arm around my neck. He laughs when I try to pick him up. Rightfully so. I fall over and land in his lap. Instead of jumping up, I take advantage of the closeness to gently palm his face. "You've helped me so many times. Please let me help you this once."

With that, he wraps his arms around me. Tremors wrack through his body, and I realize he's crying. "Oh, Jace. I'm so sorry. Whatever it is that's made you so sad, I'm here for you." Seeing him in so much pain makes me want to cry, but I don't. I decide to be strong for him.

After a few minutes of me lightly stroking his hair, he begins to talk. "You remember how I told you that my life revolves around work, booze, women, and running?"

I nod.

"Though most of that is true, it's not the whole truth. I had to work all of those extra shifts because my brother was diagnosed with cancer five years ago. I'm his only family, so I worked to pay for his treatments, his caregivers, anything he needed. He went into remission, and I worked more shifts to pay for a special vacation for the two of us. He goes out of remission, and I work extra shifts to take him to baseball games, football games, basketball games... he loves his sports. I worked my ass off to give him everything he could possibly want, but I couldn't give him what he needed. Fucking cancer. I'd have given him anything: my marrow, my kidney, anything, but he had to get it in his brain.

Radiation and chemo made him sick as a dog. False hope and vague promises about life expectancy. It's so unfair. He's all I had left in this world, and now he's gone. I held my brother as he breathed his last breath. His last words to me were, 'Thank you for all you've done for me. I love you.' I don't want his thanks. Mags, I want my brother back.

It was so painful to watch him waste away. That's why I went out drinking so much. It dulled the pain of watching him suffer. The women, well, I guess I was just looking for some comfort, but I never got it. All the rest of my time was spent with him, caring for him, sitting with him, trying to say all of the things that needed to be said before he left me.

I knew this day would be hard, but I had no idea how much it would hurt. He's only been gone for a few hours, and my life is already so empty without him. Why did he have to leave me! I save people every day. Why couldn't I save *him*? My big brother. Gone. *Fuck! It hurts so bad!"* he screams. He tosses me from his lap, and starts to punch the tree trunk. Now I know why his fists are so messed up.

I carefully get between him and the tree. "Shhh, Jace. Don't. Be mad if you want to, but don't hurt yourself."

"What does it matter?" he asks, his red rimmed eyes desperate for the right answer.

"Because it matters to me. You matter to me. A lot."

He's stunned for a moment. "I treated you like shit."

"You were going through a difficult time. I understand that now."

"I pushed you into the arms of another man, a man who tried to hurt you."

"I think you made up for that one when you kicked his ass."

"This is absurd. I need to go home." He tries to stand but buckles back to the ground.

"No way are you driving home. Wait a minute? How did you get here? I didn't see any cars in the parking lot."

"I walked."

"From your apartment? Jeez! Why come here?"

"Aside from being with Johnny, being here running with you is my favorite thing to do. I wanted

236

to be in a place that holds good memories." His words touch me.

"There's no way you're going to get yourself home in your condition. Come on. I'm driving."

"I appreciate it, but I don't think I can handle riding bitch on the back of a bright yellow scooter, Magnolia."

"If you'd bothered to answer my calls, you'd know that I don't have the scooter anymore. I drive a sedan, and I do it well."

"No shit?" Jace asks.

"No shit," I answer. Because of his weight, it's difficult to get Jace into the car, but somehow I manage. Getting him out and into his apartment is a little easier because he appears to be sobering up. While he's in the shower, I fish around his sparse kitchen and find the things I need to put on a pot of coffee. I have a steaming mug waiting for him when he takes a seat next to me on the sofa.

"I'm sorry," he says after taking a gulp.

"For what?" I ask.

"For laying all of that on you. I never should've done that."

"Why not?"

He gives me a look.

"Seriously. Why do you feel like you can't lean on me a little? Do you know how much you've helped me?"

"I did my job, Mags. I patched you up, and I got you to the hospital."

"No, you went beyond that. You saw something in me that others didn't, and I appreciate that."

"What are you talking about?"

"Like that day I showed you my before picture. You didn't act repulsed or taken aback by my ugliness."

"Because you weren't ugly."

"Jace, I was ugly."

He shakes his head.

"Do you realize that you're the first person to treat me with respect? That day in the ambulance, as I lay there with a busted up face and no teeth, you made me feel special."

"It's my job, Mags. It's what I do."

"No, it's beyond that, Jace. I'm having a hard time describing it, but it was real. A sort of feeling that I got simply being near you."

"There was no missing oxygen cylinder."

"What?" I ask.

"That day you torched yourself, and I showed up looking for an oxygen cylinder. It was never missing. I just wanted to see you again."

I shake my head. "No," I say with disbelief. "You couldn't have. Look at you. People like you don't find people like me attractive, especially when I had no hair and a wired jaw."

"People like me? What are you talking about?"

"Beautiful, gorgeous people."

"You don't get it, Mags. To me, you *are* one of those beautiful and gorgeous people. Inside and out.

I've felt that way since the day I picked you up in that art store, and I've watched as you've blossomed into a creature so beautiful that you bypassed my league long ago."

Tears begin to well the corner of my eye. "Out of your league? No way in hell. I'm just plain, ordinary Magnolia Berrybush."

"Not anymore, Mags. There is nothing plain or ordinary about you."

"Jace," I say, as I move in to hug him. He returns the embrace. I pull away then lightly brush my lower lip against his. I wait for him to respond, but nothing happens. "I'm sorry. I shouldn't have done that. It's too soon, and I don't even know if…"

Jace takes my face in his hands and pulls me toward him, kissing me with fervor that is unmatched by anything I've ever experienced. "Mags, I've never felt this way for anyone. This is new for me."

"It's new for me, too," I reply.

Jace leaves a trail of tender kisses along my face. I move to look him in the eye. "Jace, I want you to make love to me. Now."

"Mags, not this way. I don't want this to happen because you feel bad for me or because you're only just discovering that I have feelings for you. I want it to happen when and if the time is right."

I stand after taking his hand in mine. "I'm asking because it's what I want. Please, Jace. I want this for both of us."

"This is big, Mags. Once your virginity is gone,

you can't get it back. Maybe you should wait a while before making this decision?"

"I've been waiting for thirty-two years. It's safe to say I've thoroughly contemplated the decision." I guide him to his bedroom and shut the door behind us. He's working hard to keep his passion at bay; I can see it in his eyes. "Don't overthink this, Jace. It's okay. I'm asking you for this, not the other way around." I kiss him long and hard to drive my point home, and it works. He's no longer timid and uncertain; he's commanding and assured.

He stoops down to lift me in his sturdy arms, and then gently lays me on the bed. He crawls on top of me, and I bask in the sensation of his closeness. He kisses me for a long time, some short and sweet, some heavy and demanding... all of them making me want to fill an ache I'm feeling deep in my core. That feeling is amplified when Jace pulls off my shirt and unhooks my bra. He is the first man to see me topless, and instinctively I want to cover myself.

"Don't," Jace breathes into my ear. "You're beautiful. You have to know that." His lips move down my neck, across my collar bones, and down my sternum. I nearly come off of the bed when he takes one of my nipples into his mouth. He gently eases me back to lie flat and slowly releases the suction on my now erect bud. "How does that feel? Do you like it?" he asks, softly rolling it with his thumb.

"Yes," I admit. "Will you do it again?"

He smiles broadly. "Of course." He lashes his

tongue out to tease the tip of the other nipple, and once it's semi-erect, he pulls it into his mouth. He teases me by alternating sucking and pulling, and I realize there is a fire roaring down below. Everything he does to my breasts sends sumptuous sensations to my sex.

Jace stops what he's doing long enough to pull his shirt over his head. His erection pushes through the sweatpants he's wearing, and knowing that I did that to him makes me feel empowered. I wriggle out of my shorts and underwear when I notice him taking off his pants. There it is. I'm completely and totally exposed to a man, and I think I should feel intimidated and embarrassed, but seeing the way Jace is eyeing my physique, I fight the urge to cover myself.

"What a pity you don't realize how beautiful you are."

I hear what he says, but I can't stop staring at him. His chest is broad and chiseled with the slightest sprinkling of hair. His abdomen is ripped, and I grow tired of fighting the urge to touch him. I kiss his neck, and mimicking him to a point, I trail kisses down his chest and abdomen. I feel his breath catch when I get close to his Adonis' belt.

"Am I doing it wrong? Are you worried I'll break it?" I ask, suddenly feeling extremely insecure.

"No. You're doing it just right, and of course I'm not worried about you breaking it. I love the feel of your lips and hands on me," he says as I continue my journey. As soon as I touch him, he lets a loud hiss escape. "Oh, Mags. The things you do to me."

He rolls me over so that he can be on top. "I'm going touch you and while I'm doing that, I'll do a few things to make sure you're ready for this. Is that okay with you?"

Curious to see what new adventures his touches will bring, I nod. Looking in my eyes, he trails his hand to my mound and slightly cups it in his palm. I want to squirm underneath him, but I do my best to control it. While kissing me, he very gently eases his fingers into my folds, and there is one spot he hits that causes me to gasp. Still kissing me, he massages the area over and over again with his thumb until I quiver. My breathing is no longer heavy; it's coming out in quick, rapid pants. Something is happening, building from way inside. Part of me is scared of what is going to happen, but the larger part of me is worried I'll never find out. Instinctually, my hips rock back and forth against his hand, faster and faster until I feel like I'm floating. Tremors wrack my body while Jace holds me tightly. Ecstasy flows through my veins; passion fills my soul.

"What just happened?" I breathlessly ask.

"You just had an orgasm," Jace says with a smile.

"I've had orgasms before, but this one was... Can I have more like that?"

"If I do my job right, you can," Jace teases.

"It can't get any better than this."

"Trust me. It does. Unfortunately, the next part won't be so pleasant for you, but I promise that it will only be this one time, and after, it will be much better. Do you still want to do this? You can tell me to stop anytime you want me to."

"No, Jace. I want this. Please."

He gently strokes my cheek. "If you're sure."

"I've never been more sure of anything."

His fingers go back to where they were before, but this time, he uses them to enter me. The sensation is odd and slightly uncomfortable, but I trust him. After moving them in and out for a while, he positions himself on top of me and gently inserts just the tip. "I'm so sorry for this, Mags. You have to know that I never want to hurt you, but there's no other way." With that said, he pushes himself further inside of me, and I feel like I'm being split in half. Tears fill my eyes, and I, for the life of me, can't figure out why people enjoy doing this.

"I'm so sorry," Jace says over and over, as he kisses my tears away. He works himself deeper and deeper inside until he finally whispers, "That's it. That's the worst it will ever be. Are you okay?"

I nod and hug him tightly. He starts to pull out, but before he's completely free, he gently thrusts back into me. It's not as painful anymore. In fact, it sort of feels a bit numb. He thrusts several more times before asking me again how I'm feeling. I assure him that I'm fine, so he continues. His breathing quickens, and he tells me that he's close. Close to what? I'm not one hundred percent sure, but with the noises he's making, I'm pretty sure he's speaking of ejaculation.

He bites his lower lip as his entire body stiffens, and he's unmoving for several seconds. He withdraws and collapses on the bed next to me. Once he catches his breath, he rolls towards me. "How are you? Are you okay? Can I get you anything?"

"I'm fine, Jace. No regrets," I say, softly touching his face. He kisses my fingers before easing out of the bed.

"I'm not sure if you know this or not, but there is probably going to be blood. It's nothing to be alarmed about, and it won't happen every time," he says in an authoritative way.

Being that he's a paramedic, not to mention more skilled than I am in the sex department, I nod before peeking under the sheet. Sure enough, there's a stain. "Oh, Jace. I'm sorry I messed up your sheets."

"The sheets are the least of my worries. I'll be right back." He leaves the bedroom, and I hear the water running in the bathroom. He's started the shower, and it's not long before he returns to the bedroom. "Come with me," he requests.

Once I'm in the shower, he joins me, and after wetting a cloth, he slowly runs it up and down my body. I'm almost embarrassed at the amount of attention he's giving me, but instead of overthinking things, I decide to let him do what he feels is best.

He leaves to towel off, but encourages me to stay in for a little longer. I take him up on the offer and use the time to think about what has just happened. I'm not a virgin anymore, and it wasn't lost to someone like Diablo or Nick; it was lost to a kind, caring, handsome man who thinks I'm beautiful. I feel sated and content. I'm officially a woman!

Jace has made the bed with fresh sheets, and he taps it when I walk into the room. "Come rest, and I want you to take these ibuprofen," he insists.

"Jace, I'm fine," I say as I pull back the sheet to climb in. Sitting up, I look around the room.

"What?" he asks.

"Am I supposed to put my clothes back on?"

Jace laughs. "Only if you want to," he answers.

"I'll give being naked a whirl, but do you have a shirt or something I can wear if I change my mind?"

"Of course," he says, pulling a solid black t-shirt from a drawer and setting it on the nightstand. He turns out the lights and joins me in the bed. His arm snakes around my midsection, and I desperately try to sear every ounce of the moment into my memory. "What are you feeling?" he asks.

"Happy, content, grateful..." I start.

"Loved?" he asks. I roll to face him, and even though I can barely make out the features of his face in the dark, I can tell that he's waiting for an answer.

"Yes."

"Good because I do love you. I've loved you for a long time, but I wasn't in a position to do anything about it."

"I love you, too. Even when I was with Nick, you can't even imagine how many times I wanted to be with you, but you kept pushing me away."

"You understand why, don't you?"

"Of course I do."

"I'm sorry I hurt you."

"Stop apologizing. Everything worked out the way it was supposed to, but know this, your bar hopping days are over unless we're doing it together. And as for the hospital ladies who you are ever so popular with…"

"The only lady I have any interest in is lying beside me in this bed." He kisses me softly, and then moves so I can snuggle up against him. Never in my life have I ever felt more blissful than while lying in Jace's arms. Suddenly remembering what brought me here, I feel like an ass.

"Jace, how are you? Can I do anything for you?"

"No, baby. Your being with me is all I need right now. Will you stay the night?"

"Of course," I answer. "I'll stay as long as you want me to."

"I love you, Mags," he softly shares. My reply is a kiss.

The next morning, I find Jace sitting on the edge of the bed, his back to me. His elbows rest on his knees while his face is in his palms. I gently slide over to touch him, and when he looks at me, I want to cry. The hurt from his recent loss is plastered all over his face; pain is etched deeply into the dark circles that rim his eyes. I reach for his wrist to coax him back into the bed, and I notice his puffy, swollen hands. Pulling the one closest to me to my lips, I place soft kisses on each of the inflamed knuckles.

Jace rolls to embrace me, and we lie in the still, quiet room for a long time. The sound of his breathing and the beating of his heart are the only things I hear as I rest beside him.

"Did you sleep last night?" I ask.

Jace shakes his head. "No. I couldn't sleep," he confesses.

"Would you like me to leave so you can try to rest?" I ask pulling on the oversized t-shirt Jace had set aside for me the night before.

"No," he answers without hesitation. "I still don't want to be alone." He touches my hand. "Not today."

"Of course. I'll stay as long as you need me," I reaffirm. My lips lightly graze his cheek.

Jace groggily comments, "You might want to rethink those words, Mags. I'll *always* need you." My heart clenches.

"I love you, Jace."

"Mags… I love you, too," he returns before sleep finally envelops him. I don't dare move because he desperately needs the rest. He looks like hell, and I know it's because his grief is consuming him. I wish he hadn't shut me out during his brother's sickness. He admitted to having feelings for me the first day he met me. Why couldn't he have shared that with me? I could have been there for him. I could have helped him with Johnny, instead of the sole burden of taking care of a sick loved one being heaped upon his shoulders. I would give anything to rewind time and to have the confidence I lacked back then. Hell, I still lack confidence, but for me to have admitted to him that I felt a spark the first time he touched me—that could've been a game changer for the both of us.

I'm with him now and for as long as he wants me in his life; I make a personal vow to be there for him. If Jace can fall for me in spite of all of my ignorance, clumsiness, and naivety, plus the fact he didn't freak when he saw my apartment pre de-smutting—all of these things make me realize he's the perfect man. Not simply perfect to look at, although his crystal blue eyes; strong, fit body; and handsome, chiseled features do warrant a modeling contract; he's perfect for me. Except for when he was going through his darkest days, which I now know is because of the pain of an impending loss, Jace has always treated me with kindness and respect. He's patient and caring, and I realize there are no ulterior motives behind his actions. Jace really does love me, all of me.

Two hours pass, and my arm has gone from pins and needles to completely numb. The last thing I want to do is risk waking him, but my fingertips are now a nice shade of purple. He rolls over in his sleep, and I practically cry with appreciation. I massage the blood back into my arm, and the pins and needles sensation comes back with a vengeance.

"Are you okay?" Jace drowsily asks.

"I'm fine," I answer, shaking my arm out now that I know he's awake. "My arm fell asleep is all.

It's better now."

"Good," he says with a slight smile. He turns to look at the clock on his bedside table and launches from the bed. "I have to get to the funeral home to make the final arrangements for Johnny! Shit! I can't believe I overslept." He frantically runs around the room accumulating various garments from different places.

"Which funeral home?" I ask.

"Collingsworth-Fields. I can't believe this!" he says, running his hands through his mussed hair. "It's so unlike me."

He's in the bathroom, shower going in seconds flat. He doesn't even give the water time to heat up before climbing in. I search for the number to the funeral home, and the attendant who answers is very understanding of Jace's situation. She agrees to reschedule his consultation for later in the afternoon.

Jace, with a towel wrapped around his waist, has beads of water falling from his body as he dashes into the bedroom. I take the clothes he has bundled in his fist and place them on top of the dresser behind him. "Jace, it's okay. I called the funeral home, and they agreed to meet with you later this afternoon. They understand that you're grieving, and they want to do everything they can to make the process less stressful—if that's possible."

He warily shakes his head, while relief shows on his face. "I'm not sure about a lot of things right now, but the one thing I'm certain of is that I don't know what I'd do without you." The feeling I get is indescribable. After so many years of having people take care of me, it feels good to be the one doing the giving. I want to do more to help.

"Why don't you finish getting dressed? We'll swing by my place so I can get some fresh clothes, then we'll get something to eat before going to the funeral home."

"I don't expect you to go with me…"

"I'm not giving you a choice. I'm going with you. If you'd rather have privacy while the arrangements are being made, I understand that and I'll wait outside, but you're not going there alone."

He nods, then proceeds to do as I requested. While he's in the bathroom getting dressed, I slide back into my running clothes from the day before. I feel very underdressed when he comes out in black slacks and a blue button down shirt that perfectly matches his eyes. I offer to drive, but he insists that he's fine with getting us from place to place. I try to lighten the mood a bit by joking about his not needing to be scared of my driving anymore, especially since I got him home safely yesterday. He quips back about being drunk at the time, so it doesn't count. I smile, happy to know that the darkness, though still present, is no longer devouring him.

Once at my garage apartment, I invite him upstairs as I change into something appropriate, and he marvels at the transformation. I shrug. "I guess I figured it was time to grow up. I was destroyed when

Nick betrayed me, but I finally realized that it was a good thing because it made me confront reality. I've spent most of my life avoiding pain and confrontation, but now I know that it's necessary for growth. I'd stagnated living in my fantasy world, and though I thought I was happy, it's only because I didn't know what true happiness feels like. Everything about that old world was false. False expectations, false emotions, false maturity…"

"Sounds like you've done a lot of soul searching."

"I have," I admit, walking over to the bed he's sitting on so I can lace my fingers with his. "I know I have a long way to go, but I'm not scared of the journey. I look forward to it."

He pulls me close for a kiss, and before I know it, we're entwined in the throes of passion. I have only the slightest discomfort this time, and I now understand why sex is so enjoyable. We shower and dress, and after a meal at a small mom and pop establishment, Jace drives us to the funeral home. I sense his dread and reach for his hand. He gives it a squeeze to show his appreciation.

The arrangements don't take long to make, and being that there is no family needing to come in from out of town and a minimal number of friends who will likely attend, Jace insists on a brief, graveside service that will take place the following day.

I offer to give him some alone time, but he asks me to stay the night with him again. After a quick trip back to my apartment so I can pack an overnight bag, we spend the remainder of the evening talking about anything and everything.

He tells me more about Johnny and how his wife left him as soon as she found out he was sick. They had no children, and Jace wouldn't even begin to know where to find her if he wanted to. His low opinion of her seems justified to me. He shows me pictures of him and Johnny, some at games, some from their big vacation, and I'm amazed at how much they look alike. One of my favorites is of Johnny with a shaved head sitting in a hospital bed. Jace, in his paramedic uniform, is sitting next to him, each grinning broadly while holding a sign that says, "Kicking cancer's ass," and giving a thumbs up.

Jace also tells me about the car accident that killed his parents and how it was the driving force behind his career choice. It happened when he was sixteen, and Johnny was a twenty-year-old college student. They lived off Johnny's student loan money and whatever he made waiting tables at a local restaurant. Jace offered to drop out of school so he could work, too, but Johnny would have none of that. He rode Jace hard, demanding good grades, hard work, and discipline.

His brother had a successful career as a sportscaster for a local television station, but he took a medical retirement not long after being diagnosed. It suddenly makes sense why sports are so important to them, and why Jace worked his ass off to get his brother to as many games as possible.

He's sitting on the sofa, and I'm lying with my head in his lap as we talk about me and my transformation. I finally get the chance to thank him for taking the Nick situation into his hands. Jace smiles when he recalls the event. "Yeah, I'm not going to lie. It felt good giving him what he deserved. I'm pretty sure he cried."

I giggle while lazily stroking his fingers with mine. "I still don't know what happened. Big Daddy said you beat the crap out of him, but that's all I know."

"After you left my apartment, I thought about what you told me. It dominated my thoughts the entire time I worked my shift. By the time I got off, I'd stewed on it so much that I was downright livid. Fate intervened, and our paths crossed. I confronted him, and he was shocked at first and tried denying everything. He had no clue you'd overhead the conversation, but when I started spitting his words back at him, he grew defensive. He made some derogatory comments which I won't repeat. The next thing I know, he's on the ground, and I'm on top of him pounding the hell out of his face. The cops came, carted him to the hospital, and took me to jail. That's when I called your dad. He met me down there, and after I filled him in on the whole story, he had a conference with the chief.

Nick was a hair away from being fired anyway. Evidently, he'd been wreaking a lot of havoc at the department, and they'd been waiting for an excuse to let him go. We all sat down and met together, Nick included, and once your dad told him that he was going to make sure the trial would be well publicized, Nick got nervous and dropped all charges. Imagine the blow his reputation of being a bad ass would take if it got out that he was nothing more than a whiney ass bitch who cried while a paramedic beat the shit out of him."

I stop fidgeting with his fingers and move to sit in his lap where I rest my head against his chest. "Thank you for taking care of me," I say, planting soft kisses along his neck. He lifts my chin so that I'm looking in his eyes.

"Thank you for taking care of *me*," he says just before leading me to the bedroom. I'm happy to see him relax once we're beside each other, and even happier once he drifts to sleep.

Even though the day promises to be a difficult one, Jace looks much better when he wakes up this morning. The graveside service is slated for ten, so after a quick breakfast of oatmeal, toast, and coffee, Jace and I remain silent as we dress for the upcoming event. I opt for a simple black frock, and when he Jace emerges from the bathroom, he's dressed entirely in black, as well. Reluctantly, he gets behind the wheel of his truck. After a few minutes of quiet reflection, he starts the truck and slowly drives to Johnny's final resting place.

It's not until he turns the corner to enter the gates of the cemetery that he finally speaks. "What in the…" Vehicles line the path for as far as the eye can see, and a nice sized crowd is standing around Johnny's gravesite. A rainbow of flowers adorns row after row of funeral stands, while baskets filled with gorgeous arrangements are scattered all around the ground. Many of the guests are people wearing uniforms like Jace's, obviously his co-workers present to offer support. Others are in various states of dress, some in jeans and others in suits and ties.

Jace stares in disbelief at the sight before us, and I notice tears welled in the corners of his eyes. "I didn't expect..." He's obviously choked up. "I just need a second," he requests.

"Of course," I say, opening the door of his truck.

"No," he says, stopping me. "I just need a second before going over there. I wasn't expecting this. I really thought it would just be you and me here."

"You and your brother have obviously impacted many peoples' lives."

After exhaling a deep breath, Jace and I leave the truck, and hand in hand we slowly make our way to the grave site. After the brief service, I'm introduced to a steady stream of people: paramedics, supervisors, athletes, news anchors, college classmates, high school classmates, childhood friends—there is no way for me to keep them all straight. The one person I do know, Honey, looks amazing in a blue and white dress suit. I excuse myself from Jace's side to meet up with her. She gives me a huge hug.

"You have no idea how much I've been missing you," she proclaims. "Look at you. You're gorgeous, and even though the situation is a sad one, I can tell from the glint in your eyes that you've found happiness and have had at least one orgasm, if I had to bet."

"Honey!" I snap. Tugging at her sleeve, I move us further from the crowd. "Is it that obvious?" I ask.

"To me it is. I'm happy for you, Maggie. That last guy was nothing but bad news. I tried warning you about him, but sometimes in life, we need to make our mistakes to grow from them. This guy, Jace, he's the real deal. I'm a good judge of character, and he's a winner. Speaking of winners, Jerry, come meet Maggie," Honey calls to a middle-aged man with a slight spare tire and handsome face. I recognize him, but for the life of me, I can't place where I know him from.

He's very polite, conveying his condolences for me to pass onto Jace, before he walks off to mingle with some of the crowd. "He's my nose doc," Honey explains, and now I know why his face is familiar to me. I'd seen him at one of Honey's appointments. "His wife left him two years ago, so I offered to work out a special payment plan with him, if you know what I mean. He accepted, and he's been all over me ever since. Turns out, he's not a cheesy perv or anything; he's just a lonely guy with no free time for dating around. Things have been kinda tight, but I retired from hookin'. Jerry gave me a job at his office doing the filing and helping out with the phones and such. Living the legit life ain't so bad," she says with a smile. I give her a huge hug.

"That's the best news, Honey. I wish you all the best because you definitely deserve it."

"Thanks, darlin'. Looks like it's a new beginning for the both of us."

"Yeah, it sure does," I say, offering a supportive smile to Jace. He gives me a slight hand wave, which I return.

Nearly an hour passes before everyone finishes paying their respects. Once we're alone, I head back to the truck to give Jace some alone time before his brother is interred. I'm lost in a daydream when he joins me. "I'm sorry I startled you," Jace apologizes. "What's going through that head of yours to have you so distracted?"

"A little bit of everything," I answer. Jace laughs at me. "How are you?"

"I'm okay. I miss him, but I feel really good that so many people turned up to pay their last respects."

"Where do we go from here?" I ask. "Would you like to be alone? I'll understand if you do."

"No, I'm still not ready to let you go. I've been alone for too long now. I have two weeks of vacation that the company's making me take. I'm going to get away for a little while, rent a cabin in the mountains. I'd like for you to come with me, Mags. I want to hear more of your stories, learn more about you, and wake up with you in my arms each morning. What do you say?"

"I've never been out of Louisiana. It will be

another first for me. Yes, I'd love to go with you."

Jace smiles broadly, and as he eases the truck out of the cemetery gates, I can't help but think of how much I would've liked to have known Johnny if he was even half as wonderful as Jace.

****

The ride to the mountains is spent in quiet reflection, but once we get there, Jace is like a kid. Poor thing had been so consumed by work and grief that he hadn't been able to cut loose and have fun. He drags me to every show, every attraction, the theme park, and even the arcade, where I find out that my questionable driving skills are actually an asset. I smoke him on the go-cart track! We sneak kisses inside the blacklight putt-putt golf course and make love in the woods near a roaring stream. Everything is perfect until I get sick two days before we're supposed to leave.

The room is dark except for the soft glow coming from the fireplace. I'm on the sofa violently shivering while cocooned in a blanket. Jace returns from town after an impromptu trip to the grocery store for medication and the ingredients for chicken noodle soup. He kisses my forehead when he brings me a bottle of water and a couple of pills.

"You don't feel as warm. Looks like your fever is trying to break. That's a good thing," Jace comments.

"I'm so sorry I ruined your vacation by getting sick," I apologize.

"Baby, don't. It's not your fault. I hate that you're feeling this way. At least the vomiting has stopped."

"Yeah, I'm sorry for that, too. I tried to make it to the bathroom."

"I admit it wasn't much fun hosing puke out of my suitcase, but it's not the first time I've had to clean it up. Just part of the job."

"But that's the point. You're not supposed to be working; you're supposed to be having fun."

"Stop. There's nowhere I'd rather be right now. You rest. I'll be in the kitchen fixing the soup. Let me know if you need anything."

I sneeze, and it feels like my head is going to pop. Closing my eyes, I work to hold back my groan and end up falling asleep. I have no idea how much time has passed when Jace sits next to me with a steaming bowl of chicken noodle soup. I'm not able to taste much, but I know it's delicious.

Before I ask for a second bowl, I make a quick trip to the restroom, where I'm dismayed by my appearance. My nose is red and crusty, my hair sticks out in a million different directions, my eyes are puffy, and my skin is pasty and pale. No amount of makeup or primping is going to fix this mess. Sighing with defeat, I shuffle my way back to the sofa where I cover my entire body with the blanket, head included.

"Is something wrong?" Jace calls from the

recliner.

"Why didn't you tell me I look like crap?" I ask.

"Most people look like crap when they're sick. They don't want or need confirmation."

"Good point," I say, pulling the cover back far enough to expose my head. "Did I thank you for taking care of me?"

Jace laughs. "You did."

"Good, because I really appreciate it." And with that final sentiment, I'm out for the rest of the night.

Jace is standing over me the next morning, a large glass of orange juice in his hand. "How are you feeling?" he asks.

"Much better," I answer, sitting up so I can take a long gulp of the icy cold juice.

"Good. We have some things to discuss," he says with a serious tone that leaves me nervous.

"Is something wrong?" I ask.

"No. Nothing's wrong, but this is our last day in the mountains. We return to reality tomorrow. That means I'll be going back to work, and though I'll be working less now, things won't be like they are now."

I hang my head. "I guess I didn't think that far ahead. You're right. We've spent nearly every minute together since... Going back to the real world is going to suck. Hey! I know! Maybe I can become a paramedic, and we can work together!" I say happily.

"Do you remember how we met?" he asks with an amused tone. "You smashed your face when you passed out at the sight of blood. You've done it twice that I know of. I'm sorry, darling, but I don't think a job in the medical field is in the cards for you."

"Yeah, true," I mutter.

"This might sound crazy, but it's a solution to consider..."

"What's that?" I ask curiously.

"We could get married."

I spit orange juice everywhere. "What?" I ask, wiping my mouth with my sleeve.

"Forget it," Jace says. "It was just a wild idea that I should've kept to myself."

"Are you kidding me? If you are, it's mean."

"I wouldn't joke about something so serious. Maybe this will prove my sincerity?" He drops to his knees in front of me, and a black velvet box is in his hand when he opens it. My breath catches in my chest.

"Jace, is this for real? I'm sick and hideous, and this is the last thing I ever expected..."

He opens the box, and I'm awed by the brilliant sparkle of the dazzling ring inside. "It's real, Mags. I've been with lots of women... Wait, that's probably not the best way to start a proposal, and I only say it so you can know that I've been out there, and I'm certain that what we have is special. I know without a doubt that being with you is what I want, but you need to feel the same. Don't even think of accepting this ring until you're sure..."

"I'm sure," I interrupt.

"Mags, I'm serious. I want you to take your time and…"

"Yes. I love you, and I want to be with you, always. Those daydreams you caught me having, they've all been about you and our life together. It didn't seem possible to me, like a fantasy that never had a chance of coming true, but here it is. It's happening to me." I giggle. "I've wanted this since you came into my life, and that desire has only grown stronger. Jace, I don't need time. I need you."

"I'm glad I took that little detour to the jewelry store yesterday," Jace remarks as he places the ring on my finger. I can't seem to stop smiling, or staring at my beautiful new accessory.

"You bought this yesterday?" I ask. "Why? What made you decide to get it?"

"Several things. First, you being sick. As I was driving to the store, I realized that taking care of you makes me happy. Being with you makes me happy. Loving you makes me happy. It's what I've been searching for, but never could find—happiness. So, I drive to one of the scenic overlooks and have a little heart to heart with Johnny. He loved to give me a hard time. Like one day I asked him what his favorite color is, and he says, 'titian.' 'Really?' I ask, and he says, 'No dumbass. What color do you always see me wearing? What color is my house?' 'Gray,' I answer. 'There you go. See, you knew the answer all along because it was right in front of your face. Now quit wasting my time with stupid shit you already know the answers to.'" Jace smiles. "It might sound harsh, but he didn't say it to be mean. He said it because he loved harassing me. Well, anyway, that's what kept running through my head when I sat near the stream. 'Sometimes the answers are right in front of your eyes.' I look across the way, and guess what I see—a magnolia tree. It's as if it was an affirmation that I was doing the right thing. Then there was a jewelry store right across the highway from the grocery store, its parking lot lined with magnolia trees. You see, I made the decision, but I kept getting these little signs that gave me extra courage."

"Courage? Why did you need courage?"

"What if you didn't want to marry me?"

"You seriously worried about that?" I ask.

"Well, yes," he says.

"I don't think you have to worry about me ever telling you no."

"Oh, really?" he asks with a playful glint in his eye. "I *really* like hearing that." He lifts me into his arms so he can carry me into the bedroom.

"Jace, I'm sick and hideous."

"Are you about to tell me the 'n' word?" he taunts, while straddling me. He's grinning broadly while slowly unbuttoning the top to my pajamas.

"I guess not," I say with a giggle.

"Good, because I don't think it would matter at this point," he jokes.

seventeen

Six months after agreeing to become Mrs. Jace Taylor, the much anticipated day arrives. Big Daddy, who seems to have developed quite the man-crush on Jace, insists that money is no object for our nuptials, and he means it. I wanted Honey to do my makeup, but Big Daddy has hired hair stylists and cosmetologists to doll up Honey, Sunny, and me, so we all take advantage of the pampering. Once the artists finish, I'm helped into my gown, and when I see myself, tears begin to pool in the corners of my eyes. I quickly wave my hands in front of my face to keep the tears from falling and ruining my makeup.

"What's this about?" Honey asks, lightly dabbing them away.

"I was thinking about how much my life has changed in a year. I go from thinking that the only way I'll matter is by killing people, and now here I am, a princess about to marry the most amazing man to ever live."

Sunny stops primping in the mirror to look at me with surprise. "Excuse me?"

"Don't worry, it never went anywhere. Killing people was just a quick random thought."

Sunny doesn't look all that relieved when she turns back to the mirror.

"It happened a little later for you than most, but you finally blossomed," Honey says with a proud smile as she smoothes my veil. She looks absolutely radiant in a pale pink gown; it's obvious that domestic life suits her well. She moved in with Dr. Jerry a couple of months ago, and those two are practically inseparable. Jace and I have dinner with them at least once a week, and there are lots of times that Honey and I take off to go do something fun while the guys are working.

"The majority of it is thanks to you. You've helped me so much, and you've always kept an eye out for my wellbeing. For that, I'm incredibly grateful. I'm glad you're a part of my life," I say with sincerity while hugging her tightly.

When I pull away, tears are streaming down her face. "Sunny, you have raised an incredible daughter. It wasn't in the cards for me to have children of my own, so I appreciate that you share yours with me."

"Of course! My Magnolia is a gift that should be shared with the world. It took her a while to find her niche, but look at this beautiful woman. I'm so proud of the lady you've become. Your father and I love you," Sunny says.

"I love you, too."

There is a knock on the door, and Honey opens it to find Big Daddy standing outside. He's dressed in a snow white tux, complete with tails, white vest, and white bowtie. Even his shoes are white patent leather, and the fact that he carries a white cane and wears a white top hat pretty much sends his wardrobe into the outrageous category. But, it makes him happy, so I say nothing about it.

"This beauty standing before me is far too stunning to be someone I brought forth into the world. Magnolia, you take Big Daddy's breath away." I turn to look in the mirror once more before leaving with him. My long, dark brown hair is in loose waves down my back, but the sides are pulled up and held with a crystal-adorned clip to which my veil is fastened. My makeup is soft and subtle, with just a hint of rosiness on my lips, cheeks, and eyes. My green eyes sparkle under the lights, and my skin has a glow from the anticipation of seeing Jace.

"I've had a talk with my boy." Big Daddy has been calling Jace "my boy" for months now. He sees him as the son he's always wanted but never had.

"Big Daddy, you didn't say something that might make him run off?" I snap.

"Of course not! That boy is one of the best things to happen to you and this family. He's not going anywhere. No, I had a talk with him about the importance of family. I regret many of the things I've done, and not being a good father to you is one of my biggest. I hope you'll find it in your heart to forgive me, darling Magnolia."

"You are a good father, Big Daddy. How were you supposed to know that things were so bad when I constantly covered them up? That's all in the past now. I'm a different person. I'm so happy, Daddy. I love Jace so much, and I can't wait to be his wife." I hold out my hand to him. "Would you please do me the honor of escorting me down the aisle?"

"Sweet Magnolia, the honor is all mine."

We walk down a long corridor, and Sunny and Honey hustle ahead of us. The wedding coordinator gets one of the ushers to escort Sunny to her seat, while Honey is handed a white and pink rosebud bouquet. She takes her place in front of the double doors, and just before they open, she gives me a huge grin and a thumbs up.

Nerves are starting to get the best of me, and I pray that I don't vomit all over the altar. The wedding coordinator, who is unbelievably prepared, hurriedly passes me a shot of Pepto and a few sips of Sprite. It's amazing how quickly my stomach settles. Without missing a beat, she takes the drink from me, positions me and Big Daddy in our spots, and cues the bridal march.

The doors open, and my breath catches. The church is completely adorned with pink and white bows, flowers, and ribbons. Looking past the audience, I spot Jace standing next to the priest on the altar. He's unbelievably handsome in a white tux that accentuates his tanned skin. His crystal blue eyes exude absolute bliss, and I take comfort in knowing that he feels just as right about our marriage as I do.

Every ounce of me wants to run down the aisle, but Big Daddy keeps perfectly in time with the music. Guests are smiling, tearing up, and nodding as I make my way past them, and I try my best to make eye contact with each of them, but my attention keeps drifting to Jace.

When we reach the altar, and the priest asks, "Who gives this woman?" Big Daddy is supposed to answer, "Her mother and I do." However, the priest's eyebrows shoot up when Big Daddy begins one of his monologues. Gripping his lapels, he begins to pace up and down the aisle.

"My dear family, friends, and guests, thank you for joining us on such a glorious day. I was happier than a june bug on the Fourth of July the day my sweet Magnolia informed me that she'd accepted Jace Taylor's proposal of marriage. Being that she's my only child, it makes my heart swell with pride to know that through this marriage, I'm gaining a son who not only treats my daughter like the treasure she is, but has chosen a career in which he selflessly gives of his time and energy by being nothing short of a superhero. How can one not make mention of this fact? Thirty-three years ago, a child was born..." Big Daddy is interrupted by the priest's loud throat clearing. "Right, well, Sunny and I welcome each and every one of you to this joyous event, and we hope that you will join us for…" The priest clears his throat again, but this time it's much louder and more forceful. "Her mother and I do," Big Daddy bellows before kissing me on the cheek. He grumbles all the way to his seat.

I pass my bouquet to Honey and take Jace's hand in mine. He gives it a squeeze, and I give him a smile. The service seems to drag on forever because all I can concentrate on are Jace's lips and the fact that I want them on mine. Finally, the words I've been dying to hear are said, "I now pronounce you husband and wife. You may kiss the bride."

Jace takes me in his arms and dips me low while we share our first kiss as a married couple. The guests cheer, and I go weak in the knees. It doesn't matter because Jace practically carries me down the aisle as the priest announces, "I'm honored to present for the first time, Mr. and Mrs. Jace Taylor."

A stretch limo is waiting in the drive for us, and as soon as we're in the back, the driver asks if he should bring us immediately to the reception site or drive around a bit.

"Why don't you drive around a bit?" I request. "It'll give the guests time to get there and get settled before we arrive."

"Very well, madame. Congratulations to you both," he says, shutting the door. Jace raises the privacy partition and is all over me before the car is in gear.

"I've been waiting all day to have you in my

arms. It was torture watching you walk down that aisle when all I wanted to do was toss you over my shoulder and carry you out so I could have my way with you."

"Funny you should say that because I spent the entire time wishing you would."

"I guess it's a good thing I was able to control myself, or else I wouldn't get to call you my wife."

I edge closer to him. "I love the sound of that. Say it again."

"You're my wife," he says, pulling me into his arms. He tries to kiss me, but I'm in a teasing mood. To make him work for his kiss, I intend to make him chase me around the back of the limo. As though I'm playing a game of musical chairs, I quickly jump up to move to the seat across from us. I feel a sudden rush to my head, and then it's black until I hear Jace telling the driver where to park.

"Mags? Baby, do you hear me? Can you open your eyes, sweetheart?"

I want to open my eyes for him, but they feel so heavy. I manage a moan to let him know that I hear him.

"Wake up for me, Mags. Wake up."

I feel him lift me into his arms, and just as he carries me through the double doors, I'm able to open my eyes. "Hey, there you are. It's okay, sweetie. I'm here. I'm right here."

I'm deposited onto a stretcher, and Jace follows the nurses to one of the exam rooms. They ask Jace what happened, and after he tells them that I passed out in the limo, he asks me how long it's been since I've eaten.

"I can't remember," I answer truthfully.

"We'll get a blood sugar reading," the nurse says, putting her stethoscope in her ears. She takes my blood pressure and remarks that it is on the low side. She moves on to take my pulse. Another nurse hooks me up to a heart monitor, while another pricks my finger.

All of the commotion gets me nervous because I have no clue what's going on. "I'm scared," I say to Jace. He lightly kisses my forehead.

"Don't be scared, sweetheart. I'm right here, and I'm not going anywhere."

"Fifty-two," the nurse says.

"Let's start a line just in case. Jace, what's your wife's name?" the nurse asks.

"Maggie," he answers.

"Maggie, I'm going to give you some sweet stuff that will make you feel much better really quickly. I need you to swallow it for me, okay?" she asks.

I agree, and she shoots some of the thick gel into my mouth. She gives me a carton of orange juice to chase it down. The doctor comes in and rattles off a few orders. He wants them to draw a few tubes of blood so he can get a more accurate reading of my blood sugar, along with some other levels. "We're going to check you for anemia, and a few other things," he explains. I nod.

"You were right. I'm starting to feel much better already," I tell the nurse, who is now charting on a laptop.

"Great. Let's do a repeat CBG."

Someone pricks a different finger this time, and once she's finished, Jace covers my finger with an adhesive bandage. "Seventy-one."

"Excellent. It looks like you had a bit of a blood sugar issue, Mrs…?" the doctor asks.

"Taylor," I say with a smile. It's the first time I've called myself that.

"Mrs. Taylor. I'm guessing that you got so nervous and busy preparing for the wedding that you forgot to eat. Am I right?"

I nod.

"It happens more than you know. Let the drip run for another fifteen minutes. She's probably a little dehydrated, too. Do one more CBG after you d/c the IV, and if it's normal, she can be discharged."

"Yes, doctor," the nurse who is charting replies.

"Congratulations, Mr. and Mrs. Taylor," he says with a smile.

"Thank you," we say in unison.

Jace buries his face in my hair. "You scared the hell out of me," he whispers in my ear.

"I'm sorry, Jace. Thank you for taking such good care of me."

"Always. Oh! I need to get in touch with your parents to let them know what's going on. I'll tell them to start the party and to expect us in about twenty minutes. He fishes his cell phone from the pocket of his tux then steps out of the room to make his call.

"Jace is happier than I've ever seen him. You must be quite a woman. Congratulations," the only nurse remaining in the room says.

"Thank you," I say. "He's an amazing man, and I'm lucky to have him as my husband."

She smiles. "He sure is amazing. The way I see it, he's the lucky one. It's good seeing him so happy. He's always smiling when he drops off patients to us. We wondered what caused the change, but now the mystery has been solved."

"I'm so embarrassed. I'm supposed to be dancing at my reception, but I land myself in the emergency room instead."

"The doctor wasn't exaggerating when he said it happens all of the time. We get brides, grooms, ushers, parents of the bride and groom… You'll be enjoying your reception in no time. Most people won't even notice that you're late, and the ones who do will think you took a stop off for a quickie," she says with a wink.

"A quickie would've been more fun."

"I can give you two the room for a while before I discharge you," she says, and I'm not sure if she's joking or serious. I decide to go with teasing.

"Thanks, but this isn't the most romantic setting," I reply.

"Agreed," she says with a smile. "My name is

Lisa, by the way."

"It's nice to meet you Lisa. Thank you for taking such good care of me."

"It's my pleasure. I'm going to take out the IV now, then one more finger stick and you're good to go. How about you finish that carton of juice for me?" she asks.

I finish the juice, and I'm careful to look away when she pulls the catheter from my arm. No way am I risking another fainting session.

Jace returns just as they are taking the last blood glucose level, and he seems happy that it registers at seventy-eight. I'm allowed to leave the hospital, so after a quick round of thank yous, it's back into the limo we go.

Lisa the nurse was right. Everyone is none the wiser about our delayed entrance. Sunny, Big Daddy, Honey, and Jerry all rush to me, but I assure them that I'm feeling fine. Jerry tells me to find him if I start to feel bad again, and he encourages me to snack throughout the reception. I promise him I will.

Jace and I are formally introduced to the crowd, and as we gently sway back and forth on the dance floor during our first dance as a married couple, I realize that this day, even with its little hiccup, is the happiest day of my life.

We mingle for a bit, but as often as we can break away, we spend our time wrapped in each others' arms on the dance floor. "Your coat is vibrating," I say to Jace as we sway to the beat of the music.

"What?" he asks smiling.

"Your coat. Something is vibrating. I feel it."

He delves into his pocket and pulls out his phone. His brows furrow as he answers it. "Hello. Yes. Hey. Yeah, she's right here, hold on." He passes the phone to me. "It's Lisa from the hospital. She said you forgot something."

Immediately, I glance down at my ring finger. It's there, and the sinking feeling that rushed over me dissipates. "Hi, Lisa. This is Maggie. What did I forget?"

"You forgot to tell us that you've missed a period. The doctor ran a pregnancy test, and I just got the results. You're pregnant, Maggie. Congratulations."

"What? No," I stamor with shock and disbelief.

"Yep. You should schedule with an OB doc as soon as possible."

"Okay, I will. Th-th-thank you," I say, as I disconnect the call.

"What's wrong?" Jace asks. "Are you feeling sick again?"

"No," I say softly as I try to let the information sink in. "Jace, Lisa just told me that I'm pregnant. We're going to have a baby."

His face goes slack.

"You're mad. I'm so sorry, Jace. We've never really talked about it, and it's probably wrong of me to spring it on you this way…"

"Are you kidding me? Mags, we're going to be

parents! This is great news. I'm going to be a dad, and you're going to be a mom. Oh, I love you so much! Thank you for this gift! We have to tell everyone. This is too good to keep to ourselves," Jace says, practically carrying me to the stage.

He asks the DJ to stop the music and is handed a microphone. "Can I have everyone's attention please? No, Big Daddy, it's not time for the toast yet, so you can put the speech back in your pocket," Jace jokes. The crowd roars, and Big Daddy gives a hearty laugh while waggling a finger in Jace's direction. "I'm kidding. The reason I'm up here is because I thought that I'd be the luckiest and happiest man on earth when this woman became my wife. Well, I want you to know that I was wrong." Gasps flew through the audience, but then it grew so silent you could hear a pin drop.

"Jace," I scold. He gives me a grin.

"I'm the luckiest and happiest man in the world today, because in addition to being blessed with my new wife, I just found out that my gorgeous Mags is also the mother of my unborn child. I love you so much, baby." The guests go wild, cheering, laughing, and clapping, while Jace pulls me into his arms for a kiss. We're yanked apart by a line of excited well-wishers, the first of which is Honey. Sunny and Big Daddy make it onto the stage and seeing their bright, beaming faces makes me smile.

The rest of the night is a blur. We don't leave for our honeymoon until the next day, so we spend our first night as husband and wife in our apartment. Jace vows that as soon as we get back from our trip, our top priority will be house hunting. I assure him that we have time for that, but he's got it set in his mind, so I tell him I'm looking forward to it.

He helps me out of my dress, and I help him out of his tux, then we share the hunk of wedding cake Jace brought home with us. I drag my plastic fork across the top of the cake to nab one of the icing roses, but using his fingers, Jace steals it from my fork.

"Hey!" I fuss.

"Community property," he says, transferring half of the icing to his finger and letting me suck it off of it. His eyes roll back with pleasure. I reach out to do the same, but he jerks his hand back. "Nope, I want to lick my icing off here." He leaves a trail of icing that starts at the top of my breast and runs all the way underneath it. He's torturously slowly licking it off, and I find myself writhing with want.

"Jace," I gasp.

"Oh, Mags. Don't make me rush. We have the rest of our lives."

"You're right. By all means, take your time, Mr. Taylor."

"That's exactly what I want to hear, Mrs. Taylor," Jace says with a grin as he reloads his finger with cake icing.

epilogue

As I sit in a patio chair taking in the sights around me, I realize just how many lives my transformation has affected. Big Daddy, trading in his seersucker suit for a pair of denim bib overalls, is riding four-year old Johnny around his backyard on the tractor. Far as I know, he still doesn't know that I sank it in the bayou. A gust of wind blows a tuft of smoke from the bar-b-que pit in my direction, and I'm drawn back to the pig leg incident. I smile to myself when I remember the mess of that day. After all these years, Jace is still my saving grace.

Jace—my lover, my provider, my soul mate—is on a scavenger hunt with our two-year old princess, Violet. They were picking blades of grass, but now she's lured him to the azalea bushes where she loads up her tiny purse with blooms.

Sunny and Honey, both muumuu clad, are facing the bayou with easels set in front of each of them. Sunny's nude painting class enrollment has tripled since Honey's joined the roster. Her contribution?

Nude yoga as a warm up before class. I used to get grossed out when I passed by and saw all of the students sitting at their easels. That's nothing compared to the horror of witnessing downward dog being performed by a class full of naked senior citizens.

Despite her initial hesitation, Honey finally took the plunge and married Jerry. They had a quickie Vegas wedding, which Jace and I attended. She looks younger and happier since leaving the bad side of town, and I'm grateful that my friend, who has struggled and fought her way through life, gets to be carefree and happy now. Jerry is a perfect match for her. He's outspoken, funny, friendly, and couldn't care less about her past. Honey told me that he even went as far as to say he enjoys what her life experience brings to their bedroom. Evidently, his last wife was straight up missionary only, while with Honey, the sky's the limit. It was more than I cared to know, but Honey has no qualms about sharing every detail of her sex life.

Jace and Violet share a secret, and the next thing I know, she's racing towards me with a smile that melts my heart. Her dark hair and crystal blue eyes combined with her delicate porcelain skin make her look like a cross between a cherub and a baby doll. "I brought this for you, Mommy," she says, gently placing one of her blooms in the palm of my hand.

"Thank you, my sweet girl. Come see," I tell her, and after plucking a flower from her dainty little purse, I tuck it behind her ear. "Beautiful," I say, gently tapping the dark pink bloom to make sure it's in place. Violet smiles a huge toothy grin before dashing off towards Jace. How that girl loves her daddy!

"Look, Daddy! Mommy made me beautiful!"

He scoops Violet into his arms and gives her a steady stream of kisses before putting her back on the ground. She runs off to Sunny and Honey, opening her purse so each can see her treasures.

"How are you feeling?" Jace asks, sliding a chair close to me. He lifts my feet into his lap then starts to rub them.

"Great," I say enjoying the pampering. Just as I start to relax, whimpering comes from the basinet beside me. Reluctantly, I pull my feet from Jace's hands.

"I've got him," Jace says, scooping our two-month old, Carter, into his arms. I prepare a bottle for the baby, and once it's ready to go, Jace reclines back in his seat to feed him. Jace is an amazing husband and an even better dad. The love he has for his family is apparent, so much so that it's often commented on by others.

Big Daddy parks the tractor near the patio, and Johnny comes rushing to me. "Mommy! Did you see me? I drove the tractor!"

"I did! You did a great job."

"You sure did, champ. Better than your mom," Jace teases. Big Daddy, looking confused, shakes his head as he dismounts.

"Come on, Johnny boy. You can help Big Daddy check the chicken. No touching the grill though; it's very hot," he says. Big Daddy might not have been much in the father department, but he rocks as a grandpa. Johnny has been his shadow since he started toddling, and Big Daddy loves every bit of it. He spends less time in court and more time finding projects to do with his grandson. Today's is slated to be a pine cone bird feeder after dinner. He always includes Violet in the activities, but more often than not, she loses interest within the first few seconds.

Big Daddy announces that dinner is ready, and we all help ourselves to the feast. We run out of lemonade, so I excuse myself to make a fresh pitcher. Jace follows me inside. "Need some help?" he asks, washing his hands in the sink.

"I need a kiss," I answer.

"I can do that," he says with a smile. He tosses the dishtowel he's drying his hands with to the side, and with an almost catlike gait, he pins me against the counter with the weight of his body. After all of these years, he still makes me weak in the knees. "You want to make an excuse to check something out in the apartment while the others watch the kids?" he breathes in my ear.

"That's how we got the last kid, Jace," I say, laughing as I push him away.

"I'm all about the risk, baby," he teases.

"I'm not. Give me a couple more months, and

we'll talk," I say, passing the refilled pitcher to him.

"Fine," he answers with a fake pout. "I'll meet you outside?"

"Yep, I'll be there in a second."

While he brings the lemonade outside, I hastily clean the counter. Instead of going right outside the door, I hesitate for a moment. Looking at my beautiful family sends a warmth through me that is virtually indescribable. It's hard to believe that my harebrained scheme to become a serial killer has led to this. I've made my mark on the world, and it had nothing to do with infamy, just blossoming.

Romantic Suspense by
Rhonda R. Dennis

<u>The Green Bayou Series</u>

Going Home: A Green Bayou Novel Book One

Awakenings: A Green Bayou Novel Book Two

Déjà Vu: A Green Bayou Novel Book Three

Unforeseen: A Green Bayou Novel Book Four

Between Four and Five: A Green Bayou Extra (Short Story)

Deceived: A Green Bayou Novel Book Five

Green Bayou After Five: Connie's Wild Night (Short Story)

Between Five and Six: A Green Bayou Extra (Short Story)

Vengeance: A Green Bayou Novel Book Six

ABOUT THE AUTHOR

Rhonda Dennis lives in South Louisiana with her husband, Doyle and her son, Sean. She would love to hear from you. Visit her website for more information. www.rhondadennis.net.

Or write to her at:

Rhonda Dennis
P.O. Box 2148
Patterson, LA 70392

To like me, follow me, or leave a review:

Facebook: The Green Bayou Novels
RhondaDennisWrites
Twitter: @Greenbayoubooks
Goodreads Author

Made in the USA
San Bernardino, CA
07 April 2014